BRAND OF BETRAYAL

THE IMDALIND SERIES, BOOK SIX

REBECCA ETHINGTON

Published by Imdalind Press

Copyediting by
Production Management by Imdalind Press

ISBN (print) - 978-1-949725-20-9
ISBN (e-book) - 978-1-949725-23-0

Printed in USA
This Edition, January 2019

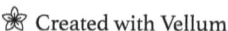 Created with Vellum

CONTENTS

To My Kids

Who are Amazing

1

JOCLYN

Wyn's attack crashed into the wall above my head. If I hadn't been paying attention it would have crashed into my head, which was clearly what she wanted given that she was cackling like some old crone.

Well, an old crone that appeared both young, beautiful, and perhaps too obsessed with the 70s.

She looked so innocent. Well, she would if it wasn't for the look of mischievous death that was wrinkling along her hairline, and the tiny bit of fire that was dripping from her fingers.

I wasn't out of the woods just yet.

Sparring with Wyn was always treacherous.

She laughed again and sent another attack right at me. The ribbon of flame smashed into the broken pew to my left and sent burning embers over my arms. The shower of sparks left little spots of black behind. My shirt, however, was not quite so lucky, each spark burned into the light cotton and spread like oil on water.

"What the heck!" I screeched, patting down the burning

fabric as I jumped away from where I had assumed I would be safe and into the open fighting arena.

"Eat fire, Joclyn! You are going down!" Wyn yelled, her voice echoing over the stone floors and bouncing off the few fragments of ancient wood furniture that was littered through the massive space.

The main floor of the cathedral may be cleared, and the walls might be covered with what could only be explained as a magical protective bladder, but when one chooses to spar against the only known person to wield fire magic you are pretty much guaranteeing destruction. And resigning to come away with a few burn marks.

Best friend or no. No one was safe.

"Teach you to take me away from Thom!"

"You mean pull you out of the dark man filled room?" I was careful to keep my voice low as I scooted behind the pew, lest she send another attack and more sparks my way. Which she totally did.

"I liked this shirt," I mumbled to myself, finally patting the last of the burning holes into submission as Wyn's laugh bounced off the sparkling walls of the cathedral bladder.

If I had been paying more attention to the ruthless assassin and not to the remains of what had been a cut geometric elephant printed tee, I would have recognized that that laugh was all trouble.

The air heated as her magic sparked, an eruption of red and yellow filling the cathedral as Wyn popped up from where she had been hiding and attempted to attack. It was the worst thing she could have done. Both her and her attack were open to view, and what she had expected to be her winning attack was useless.

My smile spread wide enough that I could have been the villain in this story. With a quick swipe of my hand, my magic pulled through the air and lifted from the ground in a wall that extinguished both her flame and her smile.

"Oh shi-" She wasn't able to say more before my attack hit her straight in the chest and with a grunt worthy of a tennis player she was thrown back, right into the magical wall that was protecting the ancient space from a rouge attack. Or in this case a flying Wyn.

She hit the wall with a smack, a ripple of light spreading away from her as the magic absorbed the velocity of her flight. She was lucky it was there. If she had soared through it she would have hit the heavy carving above the pulpit, possibly even the ancient stained-glass rosary to the side. Both things that Ilyan would not be happy to see get anything more than an admired glance.

"Not fair," Wyn gasped, the words strained as she slid down to the ground with a sigh, her body sagging as though it was limp and broken. Which of course, was an act. Wyn didn't give up that easy, and I wasn't a fool enough to think that that was all it was going to take to beat her.

"I think that's game point," I announced loudly, keeping my magic in the tips of my fingers as I vaulted over a broken pew to another, closer to where she was toppled over. Rag doll indeed.

"Claim defeat," I commanded from where I stood atop the next pew, still a good fifteen feet from her, one of my feet resting on the arm rest as if I was going to sail the thing far away from this mess. It probably looked like it with how the long golden ribbon Ilyan had woven into my braid that morning trailed around me, caught in an invisible breeze. I was sure I looked awesome. Wyn didn't even move.

"You have clearly lost. I would hate to have to finish you off, I will make it hurt Wyn."

I really wouldn't, and she knew it, either that or she

realized she looked like a fool with her face squished into the stone floor like that. Ugh. Stubborn best friend for the win.

"Besides, the faster you claim defeat the faster you can go back to pining over Thom." We both knew she wasn't pining, but it was fun to prod her.

I flicked my fingers at her as if I was firing a toy gun and sent one spark of electricity into the soft part of her neck. The attack looked like a silverfish as it cut through the air and darn it all, Wyn didn't even jerk as it zapped its way into her nervous system. I suppose in this situation most people would stomp their foot, but that was undignified for a queen in any stature, even a one month old baby-queen such as I.

Rolling my eyes at her was out, too.

"I can see you breathing, Wyn," I said, letting sparks fly between my fingers as I tightened the shield around me, ready for whatever she was about to throw at me. Because she was going to throw something at me. "I command you to accept your defeat, by order of the Quee-!"

The pew I was standing on exploded.

I had completely missed the twitch of her hand, and her palm flattening against the stone floor.

Wood splintered into the sky, hundreds of sharp points pressing against my shield like a giant needle. None were able to pierce my skin, thanks to the shield, but the shield did not do anything to protect me from the force of the explosion. As the wood flew into the air, so did I, pieces of wood twisted among my arms and legs as we tumbled and what remained of the pew below me was burned to a crisp.

Wood and body landed in a huddle, my legs flopped over my head in such a way that I had to check that I hadn't broken my back again.

I wasn't that flexible.

When I was finally able to untangle myself, pushing myself to my hands and knees with one loud echoing groan, I opened my eyes to a pair of tattered black Converse that had more than a few holes in the toes and in the soles.

"This is so not fair." It wasn't even worth trying to fight at this point. I could already feel the ground heat underneath me, besides, I had won the last four times we had sparred. I guess I couldn't win all of them.

"Concede," she boomed from above me, the fire dripped from her fingers to land on my back and burning away even more of my shirt.

"Concede? What is this a coup?" I tried to push myself up to face her, but before I could move too much, her left foot pressed against my shoulder blade, holding me down and letting her big ugly toe press through the hole in her shoe against the now exposed skin on my arm.

Great. Skin contact. Now there really was nothing I could do. I had officially lost.

"It could be." Wyn said with a laugh, her dark eyes narrowing at me in a challenge. "I don't mind taking on Ilyan. I secretly think he's scared of me."

'Okay, will you please finish her off?' Ilyan's voice boomed in my mind, his magic buzzing through our connection as it normally did when I was in distress. Wyn challenging him was only the icing in the cake. He couldn't help himself.

"Gladly." I responded out loud, Wyn's features squishing up in confusion before they widened in understanding and she attempted to scuttle away.

Too late, I didn't even need the buzz of Ilyan's magic to scare her. She saw it all in my eyes, in the bright silver that was defying her, and she took off running. I jumped to my feet, my old destroyed sneakers slipping on the ash and wood she had left behind as I tried to catch up to the treacherous snake. Okay, not that bad, but a little green garter snake maybe.

"Come back you little cheater!" I hissed as I ran after her, the sparks of my magic growing as I prepared to attack her.

I didn't get that far before my head spun, my vision popping, and yes both Ilyan and I swore in tandem.

So much for beating her butt, something more important had come up.

"Drak!" I alerted her as the magic pulsed and I fell to my knees, my vision shifting from the cathedral, to one of the many destroyed streets of Prague. Wyn was running through my sight as she had been in the chapel. Except she hadn't looked quite as scared in the chapel. Her face was panicked as she looked behind her, her dark eyes digging into me.

"The turn is near." My voice rumbled through my mind, and I was sure the cathedral. The vision shifted at the words, although instead of Wyn running through the deserted streets, it was now a man concealed by a heavy woolen cloak. My mind wanted to say it was Wyn, but there was something about the way the figure was cowering and trying to hide in the grey shadows of the ruins that didn't play to the girl I knew. Either the 70s groupie or the assassin.

"Beware the spark." The words croaked as the cloaked figure vanished in a flurry of white flakes. It took me a second to recognize it as snow, everything was so hot inside of Edmund's globe that I wasn't sure we would ever see snow again.

The snow washed the vision as it faded back to red, one quick spark of what I was sure was long blonde hair mixed in with the flakes before it was gone.

"Well, that was weird," I said as my vision pulled back to the cathedral, my hands flat against the stone as I kneeled like a dog, staring not at the floor, but at the upside-down face of Wyn, who was laying on her back between my hands, watching me.

"Yeah, that still looks freaky," she said with a smile, pushing herself to sitting as I leaned back, both of us sitting on the stone floor like children waiting for story time. "If I was going to make a horror movie, I think you would be the star."

"I'm flattered," I grumbled rubbing my temples as the sight replayed, more for Ilyan's benefit than mine.

"At least tell me it was something good, I mean, you were about to beat my ass, and then I won." She grinned broadly, ignoring the glare I was giving her, my nose wrinkled in frustration.

"You didn't win."

"You forfeit for a sight, Jos, nothing you can do about it now."

'Does anything look familiar?' Ilyan asked, but I only shook my head, as if he could see it.

"I'll just have to beat your butt in a rematch then," I said, giving her a smile and ignoring the few Skříteks who were now whispering on the other side of the barrier.

There were always a few that watched us from the other side of the barrier, someone had even gone out of their way to place a few chairs near the doorway. Normally, the space was used for training the Chosen Children that we had been rescuing and I had been healing, but Wyn and I always brought a crowd.

The Queen and Edmund's former assassin, and the only Trpaslík in our camp, going at it. I was sure it was quite a show. I was too focused on beating her butt to care. Sitting

7

here, covered in sweat with a partially burned away shirt, however, and I suddenly cared. I wished they would stop gossiping like a whole bunch of old ladies, which I guess was technically correct.

Beautiful immortals or not. They were all just a couple of old biddies, bored of the apocalyptic life.

"Oh, it's on!" Wyn said with a smile, holding her hand out for the awkward secret handshake she had insisted I learn last week.

"Consider your butt beat," I promised with a wink, using my magic to bring the mug I had left at the edge of the ring to me and filling the thing with Black Water. I would need a bit of strength after that battle, that and with how Ilyan was poking around in an attempt to decipher the sight.

'There is nothing new to see, Ilyan. I am sure it will all make sense in a few days. It hasn't started snowing on the other side of the barrier, yet.'

'We will have to ask Sain if he sees different.' He continued, his voice hard with the suggestion. If he was here I would have given him a look, even though it was clear in his tone he wasn't a fan of the idea either. As much as I hated Sain, and Ilyan distrusted him, his constant need for information and opinions in the sake of ruling often brought Sain into places he didn't belong.

Like my life.

I would be so much happier if he would step out altogether.

'You don't mean that, mi lasko.'

'Sure do. Besides, I am sure a snowflake will fall differently than it was supposed to and break every sight for the next millennium. I say we leave the old man out of it all together,' I suggested, as I grumpily took a long sip of the black water, scowling into it, which sent Wyn into a fit of giggles.

"Ilyan being stubborn again?" Wyn was prodding for more than family drama, she was all support now, my best friend shining through as she draped her arm over my shoulders.

I would give anything to spill everything to her, and complain about Sain for a few minutes. Wyn still felt like she owed him for getting her out of the dungeon in Imdalind, and as such wasn't a huge fan of my complain-fests.

She may have started standing up to him, but Sain was a tension point that I would rather not test too far. Best to avoid the Sain-subject all together.

"Do you have a cloak or something that you keep handy?" I asked, fully aware that my voice had already started cracking with the ridiculousness of the question. "Like for emergencies or something."

"I'm sorry, I think I left my emergency cloak back in the 14th century." Wyn's lips pierced together as she tried to restrain a laugh, although her eyes were completely betraying her.

"I figured as much." I was careful not to let my shoulders sag too much. Queens aren't supposed to let their shoulders sag, or at least that's what Wyn liked to remind me. Seeing as we still had an audience, the less sagging the better.

"Is that what you saw?" Wyn asked, cutting off my train of thought. "Me in a cloak?"

"Or someone in a cloak." I amended, I saw her running, and a figure in a cloak. I knew my sight well enough not to assume that both of those were one in the same. "Not that it matters. They were just running, no wicked deeds included, for all I know we are going to have cloak Olympics next summer and I was getting a sneak peek at the winner."

"I'm sorry Jos," Wyn said, pulling me into her and

9

sending a bit of black water splashing over my hands, thankfully avoiding Wyn. "That's a terrible sight to concede over. At least you can sleep easy with the knowledge that I'm going to make a great queen."

She gave me a grin and tugged playfully on the golden ribbon in my hair, the délka vedení královsk the equivalent of my crown.

"Oh, are you now?" The heavy Czech accent cut through our rambling and Wyn shot to her feet, ready to bow or nod or whatever it is that she was supposed to do. That was until she saw me still sitting below her and began crouching to try to keep her head below mine, or whatever it was she was supposed to do.

"Oh whatever," Wyn said throwing her hands in the air. "You all know I could care less about bowing. And you could care less about bowing. You hate bowing, which is great because I'm anti-bowing. And if any of our stalkers ask, I'll tell them you threatened to remove my fingers or something."

"You know I wouldn't do that," Ilyan said with a chuckle, his hand wrapping around mine as he pulled me to my feet and into him. The second our skin touched, his warmth flooded me, the sparks of his power igniting my veins like I was the track to a one man marathon.

"But I would. I have a reputation to uphold." I said as I wrapped my arms around Ilyan's waist and earned myself a look from both of them.

"What reputation?" Wyn was snickering and I couldn't even pull myself together enough to scowl at her, I was still in the middle of an Ilyan overload. "Are you turning into a gangster?"

"Do we need to facilitate a costume change before

today's meeting?" Ilyan said as he tugged on the now singed shoulder of my top. "Gold chains and a sideways hat."

"Pretty sure they only wear those in magazines," I prodded, and his smile pulled into a stubborn scowl, his lips pressed into a tight line. "But I would like to change into a shirt that is in one piece."

"Why wear a shirt..."

"I will let you two do that on your own." Wyn loudly interrupted Ilyan, my cheeks beginning to flush an electric shade of pink. "I need to change Thom's bandages before the meeting anyway." Wyn dug her toe into the ash covered floor, suddenly refusing to make eye contact with anyone. Or rather, refusing to let anyone see the shine of tears that was sliding over her eyes. "I'll see you both in a few."

She didn't look at either me or Ilyan before she bolted from the Cathedral, snapping at a few of the stragglers who were still staring at us like we were royalty. Sparring was supposed to help extinguish her pent up energy over Thom's incapacitation.

Not sure it worked.

"Darling?" Ilyan said with a laugh, clearly having read my thoughts. I refused to acknowledge him.

Yes, I know we are royalty.

"How is Thom doing?" I asked, grabbing my mug from the floor and emptying it before we left the chapel. I couldn't risk the black water dripping onto another overzealous Skřítek. Yes, it had happened before. Sometimes their bowing got a bit too eager.

Ilyan shook his head, "The quicker we get out of here the better."

"Well then, I guess we better to get to our 'Pop Edmund's Zit' meeting."

"I already told you we aren't calling the dome that, my love."

I smiled at him, he knew we were totally calling it that. He couldn't change my mind. His returning grin understood that.

2

JOCLYN

THE CROWD that had gathered at the cathedral while Wyn and I were sparring were only part of the scrutiny that my new life as a Queen had brought me.

Eyes followed me everywhere I went in a rainbow of wide and shaking color. There may or may not have been jaw dropping, whispers, or gesturing gossip that accompanied the stunned looks, with a combination that varied depending on who I was with or what crazy thing had happened the day before.

Wyn and I together were bad enough, but Ilyan and I walking together through the camp equated to something similar to the reaction you would see at a sporting event.

'Or royalty,' Ilyan provided. The crowd was already doing a good job reminding me of that.

We stepped out of the magical barrier and into what I could only explain as a sea of hair. Mine and Wyn's previous onlookers bowed low, heads and necks bared as they muttered what I recognized as the traditional greeting for royalty.

"Our King, our Queen, to you we serve."

Who says that to random, everyday people?

'Those who do not see us as random, everyday people.' Ilyan grabbed my hand as he led us through the sea of hair and into the courtyard, where more bowing and mumbling started up as if someone was revving an engine.

A really pious engine.

'It's still creepy.' I answered, knowing full well that the reason most of that ultimate creepiness existed was because some of that bowing and mumbling was directed at me. I doubt I would ever be able to accept it as normal.

'It will come with time.' I resisted a sudden need to give Ilyan a look.

'So says the guy who hates it as much as I do.'

'Accepting its meaning and purpose will come with time. I do not believe it is something you ever get used to, my love.' That time I wrinkled my nose at him, my eyebrows knitting together.

'That makes me super excited for the next thousand years.' My sarcasm ripped through our connection, and his answering chuckle filled my mind, the heat of his magic plunging against my soul.

'I am excited for the next thousand years.' His response was a tickle against my spine, and I shivered, although that could have been more from the gentle touch of his fingers against my side, right where a rip in my shirt exposed the skin.

He knew exactly what he was doing. Darn it all, I sighed like the love sick girl I was right as we reached the monastery and the sea of hair was replaced by some of the widest eyes I had ever seen.

The Skřiteks may be bowing, but the Chosen Children hadn't quite mastered that. Which I was fine with. Instead of the reverie, their heads bobbed awkwardly and they stumbled over words, or they plain stared openly at us. That's what the kid who stood outside the entry to what we were using as an infirmary was doing. His jaw was so slack that he looked as though he had a hole punched in the middle of his face. He was only a little younger than I was, his arm and neck bandaged from still healing wounds. He had managed to hole up in a jewelry store with about three others.

We had heard the screams when the Vilỳ finally infiltrated the store last week, after he and his companions had emerged to find food. They were lucky that one of the scavenging teams had been close, or we might not have been able to save them. Or worse, Edmund's men would have found them first. I had healed him a few days ago, and he was still shell shocked. The girl next to him nudging and whispering to him as Ilyan and I grew closer.

"My...my..." He stuttered around the words once we were within earshot, clearly uncomfortable.

Made sense, I was raised as a boring mortal too and hearing everyone call Ilyan 'my lord' in the beginning had been bizarre. I had never called him that, because it was weird.

That and he hated it.

That and stubbornness. Although his or mine I wasn't sure.

"Yours." Ilyan answered aloud, giving me a sassy side glance that sent my stomach into a paratrooping air show.

Ignoring Ilyan and his stomach swooping smile, I stepped past him and right to the kid whose eyes looked about ready to pop out of his head with each step I took.

"Hi there. It's nice to see you out and about," I said, realizing too late that I not only spoke in English, but that the greeting was neither very queenly or logical. I wasn't sure if he had understood me, but the guy now looked like he was ready to pass out. Because Queen.

"How are you feeling?" I gave Czech a try that time, but I wasn't sure if I had even said anything correctly, but at least he understood me that time.

The kid and his friend exchanged another look, their eyes growing even wider as Ilyan came up behind me, his tall frame towering over all of us by a foot.

"Bet...better." Or, I think the wide-eyed kid said 'better', the stuttering Czech made it even harder to understand him. The warmth of Ilyan's hand against my shoulder, however, was a comforting affirmation that I was on the right track.

"I'm glad to hear it," I began, speaking slow and carefully trying to find the right word. "You guys escaped quite the predicament. I'm glad we found you."

I smiled brightly, trying my hardest to look like the friendliest, most human-like queen possible. The kid however, was beginning to look like his eyes were going to pop out of his head, his lips pulling into a tight line as he tried to restrain a laugh. The girl beside him had melted into a loud roll of laughter that caused me to jump, Ilyan's only partially restrained chuckle added to the sound and I rolled my eyes.

An act which was justified given the situation.

"Great," I grumbled, not even bothering with the Czech now. "What did I say?"

"That his dumpling is quite the predicament and you are glad to have eaten it." Ilyan could scarcely get the words out, I had to pick most of that out of his head.

"Well, damn." I patted the now giggling kid on the shoulder, giving my own mumbled apology and stepping through the entrance of the monastery-hospital thing. "Of course I fall in love with the guy who rules the country that has the hardest language ever."

He gave me a look that said he was ready to challenge me, but instead wrapped my hand over his, pulling me closer to him as we walked down the tile hall toward the large wing on the other side of the complex. The building was beautiful with so many hidden alcoves and secrets that it had become one of my favorite places in the castle.

Even now, as we walked down the long hallway, passing each of the high windows, and the old doors that had been carved in centuries long since forgotten, it felt safer than any other place that I had been today. Probably because there were no bowed heads, muttering voices, or wide eyes. There was no Wyn, ready to battle me down like we were in a video game. It was just Ilyan and I, wrapped in a privacy that we rarely found outside of our tiny room in the sanctuary.

I took one deep breath as we walked through the red tinted sunlight that was streaming through the high windows, the heat of Edmund's zit feeling like a sauna against my skin. I froze underneath it's warmth, pulling Ilyan to stop and guiding him around to face me, the brilliant blue of his eyes sparking with the light gold that I had only seen a few times before.

"You don't have to try so hard, my love. They all know you are learning." Ilyan whispered as he stepped closer, pushing some of the hair that had come loose from my braid behind my ear, his fingertips grazing the edge of my mark. My skin heated even without the contact, my magic running its own supercharged race through my veins as it flooded to my mark, desperate for the connection.

I'm glad the touch ended there, I wasn't sure I could take much more without major repercussions. My magic was still super-heated from sparring with Wyn, and I happened to like these windows. They were big and old and not cracked down the middle because the King and Queen were having a make-out session right beside them.

"If I am going to be queen I am going to be the most normal every day queen that ever was," I said, stoically ignoring the way my stomach was fish-flopping.

"You are making the proclamation as though I expected anything else." Ilyan wrapped his arm around my waist and pulled me against him. The scent of magic and pine that always followed him around assaulted me in a pleasurable wave that was making it hard to stand or even walk, even without the differences in our heights.

"I'm sad I am going to miss the gold chain and sideways hat, however," Ilyan whispered against the top of my head before he kissed it, his magic cracking down my back in sparks. Ice pricked up in goose flesh as though I had been plunged in cold water and I quickly restrained the chihuahua level shiver that his touch was giving me.

"I am sure we can arrange another time for us to go all gangster on each other," I quipped. Ilyan was giving me such a look it was clear his mind had gone somewhere else than the karaoke party I had envisioned. Yep, that time I totally shivered.

'Get your head out of the gutter, Ilyan,' I chastised where no one could hear. Yes, the hallway appeared to be deserted, but I wasn't about to take any chances.

"Not in the gutter. Just on a beach. With you. In my arms. Against me," Ilyan whispered each word slowly, lifting me against him as the hot breeze of his need tickled my ear. His teeth pulled at my lobe, sending a million more waves of ice, and heat, and magic over my skin.

"Ilyan," I groaned, grateful when he placed my feet back on the floor. Although the gratitude vanished when my shaky legs were unable to support my weight and I tumbled head first through the large set of double doors and into the new arrivals wing of the monastery.

The only 'new arrivals' that were in here were still unconscious, but the Skříteks and the few Chosen Children that were awake and working turned in unison to give me such an array of expressions they might as well be a living 'rate your pain' scale that you see at a doctor's office. Well, that the mortals do, I wasn't sure any of these guys would know what I was talking about.

"I guess I shouldn't have abandoned the gangster hat quite yet," I said as I pulled myself to standing. Everyone was staring at me. I was sure the bits of magical residue on my skin and torn shirt was helping me to maintain that whole sane queen look.

Ilyan however, laughed riotously as he strode passed me, his fingers grazing over the edge of my mark as he made his way to Risha, who was counting gauze and tree roots and some gnarly looking purple flower that might have been pulled from a trash bin.

Everything was scattered over a table in the corner, the makeshift storage system in front of her looking woefully empty.

Crap. We were going to have to plan another supply run.

As his second, Ilyan always met with Risha before the meetings to go over schedule and itinerary and other things that I could pick out of his head later.

War planning wasn't my favorite. I had other things in this room to occupy me, anyway.

"Hey Deterim," This guy smiled with my casual greeting, he was too used to me by now. "Anything I need to be aware of?"

"Nothing new in the last few days." Deterim lowered the

clipboard he had been inspecting and looked over the beds that were perfectly placed through the room. Most of them were empty, but the few that were filled were occupied by those that I had already healed, their magic already buzzing healthily through their veins. I could feel it in the air as though it was an electrical current, the soft heat welcoming in its own way.

It was definitely better than that smell of blood and bark that usually drenched this room. The city was still full of survivors after Edmund's attack. Many were hidden away, but one step outside and they were bitten by the Vilỳ, leaving us in a race against Edmund's men as to who could get there first. Who could save them. We had found thousands, but I couldn't help but think that there were more hidden in dark corners and alleys. Thousands more that we needed to save from Edmund and whatever he was doing on the other side of the barrier.

"I know there is a team going out later tonight, but I will fetch you if anything happens, my lady," he said with a smile that might have well slapped my nerves to life. Yeah, that was never going to be any easier.

"That would be great, Deterim, thanks."

He smiled again, making me sure that that was not something that 'someone in my position' would normally say. I didn't care.

His mention of a team going out smacked against the side of my head, the brief sight that had cost me my win coming back into play. Wyn running through the city, someone in a cloak.

It didn't make any more sense now than it did before. And that weird flash of blonde hair didn't make any sense. I shook my head in an attempt to dispel the images, the end of my braid tapping against my neck as the golden ribbon trailed behind me like a tail.

'How did Deterim know we were going out tonight?' I asked to Ilyan as he made his way through the beds back to me, a slightly red faced Risha on his heels. *'And what in the world did you do to Risha?'*

'Risha is embarrassed of some romantic affections she has for someone close to us. I brought it up,' He said as he reached me, his eyes smirking even as his lips pulled together. *'Our mission is concealed. Perhaps he got the dates mixed up for next weeks supply run? I wonder if that's the run that you are seeing, my love. Wyn on a mission in the city?'*

"With how scared she was, I really hope not," I said aloud as we stepped through the door, and back out into the hall, which was as devoid of people as before. It was so quiet that you could hear the squeak of my trainers and the tap of Risha's kitten heels with way too much vibrato.

"How scared *who* is?" Risha asked in English that was as broken as my Czech.

"My brain," I responded with a huff.

"You know," Risha said, moving to open the door open for Ilyan and I. "I may join Wyn's team of banning you two from doing that. It's weird."

"So is seeing the future in your head," I said with a shrug. "I'll explain at the meeting."

Risha seemed pacified by that and moved to the side, letting the red light stream into the hallway like some kind of red carpet. The analogy didn't seem very far off. I braced myself for the bowed heads and mumbling again. Keeping my chin up, I took one step into the red light, and froze.

Everyone was gone. Normally there were a few that hovered around the doors, waiting for us to reappear so they could continue their bowing. Sometimes I thought it was all they knew how to do.

The steps and the courtyard was empty. Even the boy that I had made a fool of myself in front of was gone. It was just the heavy stone courtyard, the tall white walls of the apartments and the towering spires of the cathedral. I was sure that if there was wind inside of this zitty dome that I could have heard it whisper through my hair.

Even the lone step I took out of the monastery was like a slap against the inside of my skull. Okay, so I had somehow stepped into a sight. I wasn't even sure how that would work, seeing as I had never done it before, but I couldn't think of another explanation.

"This is not a sight, my love," Ilyan whispered, his fingers drifting over the long golden ribbon that was trailing over my shoulder as he stepped passed me, "but I think I know what is going on."

A weird darkness had taken over his voice as he turned toward one of the large fountains on the opposite end of the square, and the crowd that was gathered there.

"What in the world is that?" I asked, my mind went through a million possibilities in a second, none of them good, and none of them wanted, before a shaggy man in what appeared to be a tattered suit jumped onto the lip of the fountain, his arms waving over the crowd as he spoke to them. Forget the nervous twist in my stomach, the twist had turned to stone and taken my heart right with it.

"Why does he look like he's about to lead them all to Zion?" I folded my arms over my chest as I glared at the old man, not that he could see it from where I stood. "I think I would take a Vilÿ attack over this."

"You would take a Vilÿ attack over your father and his

gifts?" Risha asked, her voice so awed that it twisted deeper through me, bile threatening to break over me.

"This is so much worse than a Vilỳ attack." I was in full on pissed growl now.

Ilyan gave me a warning glance, I was a being a bit too open with my disgust of my father and I knew it.

Too bad it was about to get worse. My heart dropped as he brought someone from the crowd onto the lip of the fountain with him. I recognized the newcomer at once, the kid that I had complimented his dumplings on minutes before. He looked even more awestruck than when I had approached him.

Sain's gestures grew more wild as he talked to the crowd, the excitement growing as he produced one of the heavy mugs that had become the source of my only food. Of any Drak's food and sight and magic.

"What in the world?" I stepped forward, ready to run to the crowd and pull the kid away from him and whatever he was about to do. I may not be fully trained in that side of my power, but I knew that this could only spell trouble.

That was freakin' it!

"Joclyn, don't!" Ilyan called from behind me, but I was already charging toward the crowd ready to bust through them and break up this nonsense.

I had only reached the edge of the group when Sain dipped his thumb into a mug of water. The water that was harmless to us, and poison to any non Drak that may touch it. The old man didn't wait before he pressed his now wet thumb against the forearm of the kid and sent him screaming.

And me to my knees, my vision going black.

3

ILYAN

JOCLYN FELL to her knees as though it was in slow motion, her body crumpling until she knelt on the ground like she was joining the throngs in worshiping her father.

That should have been my first clue that something had gone horribly wrong.

The crowd called out in alarm, but not for the plight of the queen, but for the display that Sain was creating. The fool's eyes had drifted to black, the water in the fountain behind him lifting up in a pillar of swirling lights that, to those who hadn't seen it, looked like something lifted from the bowels of hell. And most of those in the crowd hadn't seen the magic of a Drak before. The gasps of awe turned to terrified screams, it was clear that Sain had gone too far.

He hadn't prepared them for what they were going to see, for what was about to happen, and they were terrified.

This was not the way we had discussed training those bitten by the Vilỳ!

Now it was me that was ready to charge through the crowd, my magic and temper roaring to the surface as the colors in the water shifted into an image. Screams turned to gasps of amazement, as a face took shape, the mirror of the boy next to Sain clear in the surface of the water.

Joclyn's back arched as I was about to pass her. The motion was identical to Sain's as their magic flared, joining them together in sight. Her power pulsed through me the same as it always did, although this time it was strong enough that I was nearly brought to my knees.

Drak magic was permeating in the air like a snow drift, the pressure so heavy that I wasn't sure how all of these Chosen and Skříteks weren't feeling it.

How they weren't drowning in it.

My nerves sparked with electric energy as the sight pounded against the back of my skull, my connection with Joclyn allowing me to see as she did. Usually I would hold her close, let our magic mingle and watch the vision unfold as I peeked into the future, and in some cases the past, with her. My worry for her fought with my temper, the anger winning out when, instead of the deep booming voice I had come to expect from a sight, both Sain and Joclyn began to scream. The high pitched shriek from my mate was unexpected for those at the back and they all jumped, spinning around to face Joclyn who was now twisted like a child in a horror movie, her joints bending at weird angles as the scream ripped from her throat.

The look was terrifying, and even though my first instinct was to jump before her and block her from view, I knew she was safe. Risha was rushing to her side, kneeling beside her as the Drak magic overtook her. Everyone around her was staring in terror at the two of them, unaware that this was how Drak magic worked.

Sain was a fool.

Joclyn's scream faded into loud popping noises, the sound almost a gag, as if the sight was trapped in her throat.

Odd, seeing as Sain was speaking as clearly and openly as he always did in sight. His deep, booming voice spread over the courtyard, drifted through the windows that were still being repaired and dragged Skříteks and Chosen out of buildings.

"At the edge of night and day, the battle begins, the battle will stay."

The crowds swelled as the image in the fountain shifted from the smiling boy to the red tinted city, four people in long dark cloaks walking through the scarlet world. None of them were recognizable, except for the glimmering gold of the ribbon that trailed from behind the hood of one, the délka vedení královsk a glimmering gold amongst the red.

"You must keep... away. Stop them... stay." Joclyn's voice was drowned in the clicks and gasps as she lay contorted on the ground, Risha's shocked expression meeting mine as I turned back to where she sat protectively around my wife.

Her words repeated in my head as they mumbled past her lips, my anger slowly melting into confusion, and then fear.

That was not what Sain had said. The words of a Drak always went together, both in tone and words, but this was such a drastic change that Joclyn might as well have been having a completely different vision.

It wasn't the words that had always gone together, it was the sight as well. And that seemed to be as broken as a cracked egg. The flashes of Joclyn's sight that I allowed to fill my mind didn't seem to match what was streaming through the fountain like a bad copy of a 1980s horror movie.

Joclyn was seeing a man surrounded by children, his face spread into a smile.

The water of the fountain was painted red as blood spread over the street they were running down, one of the cloaked people falling to the ground, although there appeared to be no assailant around them. It was as if the wall of water was attacking. The boy who had been branded with Black Water, the boy that Joclyn was seeing with a happy family, contorted in the water as he screamed, as he ran from the wall, and whatever it was that was killing them all.

"There is no future in the truth of a man, for their childish magic will lead to an end."

Sain's voice continued, the sight shifting as though it had somehow lost its connection, the same image repeating again, except this time the boy was felled with the rest of them, a bright red streak of blood seeping through the cloak on his back. The crowd erupted into a weird combination of gasps, cheers, and screams as the image changed again, this time to Prague, but without the giant blob that was covering us all.

Even that shuttered, back to the wall, to a haphazard army that was thundering into the city through the barrier and five lone shapes that stood facing it. That image matched up. For a spark of a second both the sight in the water and the images that were plaguing my mate were the same, and then they were gone. Replaced by images of danger and joy and death that came so fast that it was as though we were watching TV with a remote happy toddler.

Sain was forgotten as I sprinted back to Joclyn who now appeared to be having a seizure on the ground. Her body shook as she gained the attention of everyone around us, their focus torn from the fountain of Sain's sight, to the queen who had gone back to screaming, rogue words slipping in between the shouts.

"Attack... take the... like ants they come..."

Her magic was so supercharged that the second I

touched her, our magic ignited as though I was touching a live wire, pushing magic and sight into my mind in a wave.

"Joclyn," I gasped, my spine straightening as the power began to subside, my voice faltering both aloud and in her mind as I tried to see through the onslaught of images. "My love, what is going on?"

The only answer I received was screaming, and the more she screamed, the more heads turned to her. People were running across the courtyard now, drawn to the drama as though they were moths and flame. I could have screamed thanks when I saw Wyn tear through the crowd to reach us, busting through the worried and entertained throngs like she was her own personal bulldozer.

"I've got her. You go stop that bastard before I do," She hissed with a nod to Sain, who was still spouting nonsense from the deranged pulpit that he had built. "I'm sure you will end things a bit eh... shall we say cleaner."

The smile she gave me was one I hadn't seen in centuries, and I wouldn't hesitate to say I didn't miss it.

The old Drak was now standing before the pillar of water as though he was a god, his hands outstretched as his tattered suit rippled in wind and water. Seeing him there, his black eyes staring to the sky, made me think that perhaps sending Wyn to him was the better idea.

End it quick. Clean. And with maximum restraint.

I was up and racing as the image behind him shifted to another dark cloak, this one a lone figure sprinting through the darkness of night, streaking past the destroyed buildings of Na Prikope.

I had barely made it through half the crowd, but that made me freeze.

This I had seen.

Yes, I had grown up in this town, everything about it was

familiar, but this moment I had seen less than an hour ago in Joclyn's sight. I spun to her, but she was still trapped in sight, her body calmed as she heaved, her exhales deep as she pushed herself to stand, moving like one possessed. Her eyes were still swathed in the black of sight as she stared past me, past Sain, her focus on something far away.

"Follow your heart for the other half is here, and in the dark it will flourish." Sain's voice was a boom, but again Joclyn's did not match it, her words were more like a solitary warning than the grinding threat that came from behind.

"Destroy the mice or the dark will flourish." I wasn't sure anyone else had heard her, the deep words ran through my head as they passed her lips, the spark of the sight following with it and showing an attack right beside the barrier. Although this time it wasn't the cloaked figures fighting an invisible nothing as Sain had shown, it was the five of us fighting Edmund's men, dozens of them popping through the barrier like it was nothing but a soap bubble. Streaming toward us like mice.

Destroy the mice.

Joclyn's eyes were slowly returning to their piercing silver as Risha and Wyn huddled around her, both of them supporting her weight as Ryland bolted across the courtyard, obviously alerted to the dissolving mob that this crowd was becoming.

Nodding toward my youngest brother, I motioned for Risha to follow me. I had no need for my guard but it was the illusion of control I needed now, and Ryland and Wyn could take Joclyn to our quarters, provided she wasn't too stubborn to allow them to take her there.

'I'm not going anywhere, Ilyan. I'm fine. I'm staying here.' Joclyn's voice was as strained inside as she appeared outside. Her eyes, however, were as defiant as always. Little

sparks of silver that met my gaze, not even flinching as Risha and Ryland traded places, Ry easily hoisting Joclyn up to hold her against him, leaving Wyn to take over crowd control

'You aren't going to want to be here for this, Joclyn.' I made sure to use her name, to drive the point home. But her gaze didn't even flinch from mine, she only narrowed her eyes defiantly.

"Like hell if you think I am going anywhere, Ilyan." Her voice was pure fire in my head as she yelled.

Ryland laughed at her challenge, the sound as out of place as Joclyn's screaming.

"Don't be a fool, brother," Ryland called after me, helping her to find her feet. "You know better than to prod that."

I did. And every bone in my body knew that he was right.

"My beautiful, stubborn Queen." The words were lined with the growl of my temper as I turned from her and pushed my way through the crowd before she had a chance to follow me. I only hoped Ryland could keep her back for a few minutes more.

"The power of sight is one of the oldest magics that our kind holds, it's powers so rare that..."

"Sain!" I cut him off with a boom, I wasn't interested in letting this foolishness continue much more, and it had already gone on too long. "What do you think you are doing?"

"My Lord! I am so glad you could join us. I decided it was time to show our new Chosen the strength of magic a true Drak has." His smile was wide and welcoming, but the use of my full title, as well as the slight dig against Joclyn, was tugging at my temper, my muscles rippling over my back.

He has always been arrogant, lately he was bordering on incorrigible. I needed to end this and get back to Joclyn. I was too frantic, too angry, and quickly becoming dangerous.

"Such decisions should be made by those above you. This display is not wise, Sain." I tried to pull him away from the edge of the fountain and the crowd.

"These children wished to see the true power of a Drak. So many of them have expressed wonder at having one of the firsts among them. I only wished to show them of my power, of the true power that was birthed from the well of Imdalind."

Good to know that Sain's arrogance was thriving in the crowd of unsuspecting children, newly born to magic. He knew that just the creation of black water in a mug would send them talking for weeks, and yet he chose to reveal the full power of sight, tapping into Joclyn in order to make it work. Before, sights of that caliber would take the strength of a dozen Drak to accomplish.

No wonder Joclyn was reduced to screaming, her body exhausted.

'I'm fine, Ilyan,' She interrupted, her magic sparking as it moved closer. It was a fool's hope to think that she would stay out of this. *'Yes, it was.'*

"There are better ways to do this, Sain, than to tarnish one of our main water supplies." I was careful not to touch the damp stone as I pushed myself to the ledge of the fountain beside him. I had been burned with the stuff far too many times for another burn to matter, but I was not interested in letting this man see into my life too closely. Future. Past. It didn't much matter to me.

I wasn't going to even look at Black Water if he was in the vicinity.

"The water is fine, Ilyan," Sain announced, far too loud

and boisterously than was strictly necessary. He held his hands up, spraying a bit of the residual drops over the crowd who shrieked in excitement, obviously not understanding what was going on, or the danger that they were in. "My magic has returned it to its true state, ready for more sight..."

"There will be no more sights, Sain." My voice was hard enough of a warning that I hoped he would heed it and back down from whatever game he was playing.

"That is true," The joy in his voice fell away and I tensed, eyes narrowing as I stood over the man. I knew what was coming next. "The power of my sight continues to struggle and fade after so much of it was damaged."

"These opinions are not meant for this audience, Sain." It was becoming much more difficult to control my frustration against him.

I wanted nothing more than to push my magic into my voice and force him down, force him to obey. Instead, I kept my arms and hands calm against my legs, even though every muscle in my back was pulled into tight little braids, the tension invisible to all who didn't know me. But Sain, Sain knew me.

"This nonsense can wait for a more appropriate time."

"It is not nonsense your majesty, my daughter--"

"We can talk about this later, Sain," I cut him off before he could say anything worse about the Queen, especially before so many people. I was already shaking with anger. "We must discuss the time and way to expose those new to our world to our magic, to our customs. And learn when to keep opinions to ourselves."

The last words were low, and just for him, his eyes flashing with a dangerous darkness that may have sent anyone else into a cower. He was lucky Joclyn was not standing beside me, or else the look would end in rage. As it was, I was only barely able to control myself.

"You would censor my magic, My Lord? You would censor the magic of those new to our world? They should be able to know all of our world, of their new worlds, and of the choices of others!"

"I censor nothing. There is, however, a time and a place for such things." I was speaking through my teeth now, but still, he did not heed the warning.

"As the first of my kind I would entreat you to know of the dangers of putting them under lock and key, My Lord." He sneered, the title heavy and dead on his lips now. "They deserve to know all there is about this world of magic, and if I am the only one who can show them the power of the Drak, then I will make it my duty to do so."

"You are not the only one with the power of the Drak," Joclyn's voice was powerful, strong, and if I wasn't so proud of her for standing up to her father, I would be upset that she had followed me to the front.

The heat of my love swelled alongside the violent spark of silver in her eyes. She was every bit the queen that she tried to pretend she wasn't, the power that was seeping off her like a wave of heat that people backed away from, leaving a path for Wyn, Jos, and Ry to walk down.

She was a powerful Drak, the air around her rippled and bowed down to her as she stepped towards her father with such command that even he stepped back, his heels slipping off the back of the fountain and sending him tumbling. The man caught himself, but not before a wave of snickers moved through the group.

"My sight is as strong as yours, Father, and often sees things that yours refuses to see." Sain faltered with the tiniest stutter at the strength in her voice, and every muscle in my shoulders straightened in warm joy at seeing the power in her.

Well, until Sain laughed with a rough, scratchy sound that was nothing but mockery.

"I am of the first, my daughter, my power sees nothing but the truth. You simply have not been trained enough to know the ways of a Drak, of our magic, and of its full strength and ability." The condemnation in his voice pulled at me and I stepped closer, towering over the fool with as much warning as I could fit into my eyes. He did not care, however, and plowed on, the focus of the crowd swinging between Sain, Jos, and I with wide-eyed ping-ponged focus. "You defied the sight from centuries before you were born that showed of your death, you denied your heritage and your breeding. If you wish to be a powerful Drak, we must train you, teach you of what is right."

"That is enough!" This time I pushed my magic into my voice, the power sliding through the air and infecting not only Sain, but everyone who had gathered around the fountain.

The Skřítek warriors fell into pious apology. The Chosen, however, looked terrified. Just as they were overwhelmed by the full range of Drak magic, the deep power of their king was sending them into a tizzy. This control was something I abhorred, but right then it was creating a bigger problem than I anticipated. The twitch of Sain's smile as the last of this laugh faded away was making me uncomfortable.

'They will understand, Ilyan.' Joclyn soothed into my mind, her magic pulsing through my veins. *'We must help them understand.'*

"I will not allow any of this, Sain." I was careful to keep the magic out of my voice that time, even though my words continued to roar. "The Chosen must be introduced to our world slowly..."

"Your father was not introduced slowly," Sain interrupted, his voice loud enough that everyone could hear. In fact, with the way he turned and roared it was clear that he wasn't talking to me at all. "We showed him everything from the moment he woke from his kiss of the Vilỳ. The wonders of magic were open to him. From Skřítek, to Trpaslík, to Vilỳ, to Drak."

Sain looked from me, to Joclyn, to Wyn and finally placed his hand on his chest with so much reverence he might as well have been worshiping himself. There was a high chance he was, and the action sent my blood right back into a boil.

"There was none of this coddling as you would do to the Chosen. I see what that has done to my daughter." The word had as much hatred behind it as my title, even though he looked at her like he was going to worship her as well, his head bowing slightly.

'Can I punch him now?'

'I highly doubt that would end well, Joclyn.'

"Now I see what that choice to coddle her has done to the magic of the Drak."

His reverence faded, his face falling into dejection as everyone whispered, but not in the mumble of acceptance. This time it was in question. In worry. Perhaps in fear. Each look cut through both of us, and while I tightened my jaw in frustration, Joclyn's fists tightened against her jeans. Her two pseudo bodyguards were beginning to look nervous.

Ryland was, anyway.

Wyn was downright entertained, her face spread into a smile as though she was waiting for her turn.

'Do not rise, my love,' I pleaded, but the angry pulse of her

magic was so high that I could tell there was no stopping her.

"Ilyan did not coddle me!" Joclyn's voice was low, dark, each word spoken with power as she broke away from Ryland who was trying to pull her back as she rushed the stage. "He pushed me, he trained me..."

"And then he wed you and he bed you." The punch of his words slammed against my chest as gasps and whispers overtook the crowd. Even Jos froze in her charge, stumbling right back into Wyn who was glaring daggers at Sain, her pain radiating through me.

Gathering her into my arms in comfort was out of the question given the vile words that hung in the air.

The man truly was arrogant if he thought he could speak to my mate that way. Luckily, Wyn cut in before my temper rose and I did something I would regret.

"What's it to you, old man?" Wyn's voice was a cross between a snap and a laugh, as she tried to muscle her way in front of Joclyn. Joclyn pushed her back, however, the queen's jaw tight as she breezed past the Skříteks and jumped onto the fountain between me and Sain, facing her father head on.

This time I wouldn't let my awe of her get in the way of my protective need, although I would not wrap my arms around her as I wanted to.

"It means everything to me, Wynifred! It means everything to you and to all of us. Everything is connected. And the longer she remains untrained, my sight continues to suffer." Sain took one slow calculated step closer to her and I threw proprietary to the side, wrapping my arm around Joclyn and pulling her against my chest. I fixed Sain with a glare of warning, but the fool didn't follow, or rather he didn't see with how intently he was staring at his daughter.

"Enough!" I boomed, letting my magic drift through the world and terrorize the Chosen even further as their tongues and bodies were instantly bound under my command.

"I agree, My Lord," Sain said, suddenly penitent, the low calm that normally followed him around returning to his voice. "Perhaps I have been unfair to my daughter. The same power runs through her veins. Perhaps she would like to show her people of her strength and join me in sight."

We had heard this speech before, but he wasn't talking to us. Sain had turned to the audience, the transfixed crowd stepping closer.

"They have seen the power I hold, show them the power of their queen!"

"This is neither the time..." Anything I had been planning to say was drowned by the roar of the crowd, screams and cheers of eagerness and excitement breaking through my bind and lifting through the air and wiping away any control I could regain from the crowd.

Well, not without scaring them. Not without becoming the King my father was. I wasn't interested in letting that happen.

'You should have let me punch him when I had the chance.' Frustration dripped in her voice as she stepped right up to Sain, his chin high, her silver eyes blazing.

She was sure, confident, and entirely in over her head. She had never performed magic of this caliber before, she had never even seen it. Of course, she had done so much that we had never known to be possible.

I was sure she could do this, and it would be wonderful

to see her stop Sain in his boisterous display. But now was simply not the time.

'Do not give into him and his games, my love.' I was attempting to be persuasive, but I knew there was no stopping her. Wyn had even planted herself on the front row, shaking her head with a half amused grin.

'Maybe I want to play too.' The power bled from her voice. I wanted to pull her back, to protect her from whatever Sain was doing. But protecting her did not mean smothering her.

Besides, it was always amazing to watch her.

'Then show him. Teach him not to doubt you.' I placed my palm on her back, the magic of our connection swelled before she took another step toward him.

"Wonderful, perhaps the king would be so inclined to allow you your first attempt. Surely the combination of your magic will make it easier for you to see into his fate and share what you see?"

The confidence that had been drifting from her like a fine perfume faded in a sigh of shock that twisted toward me, her shoulders drooping as her fear bled into me. I attempted to push through our connection, to see what beast had come to sit on her chest, but found the way blocked, by her.

'Joclyn, what is going--?'

"My daughter," Sain said, his hand curling around her shoulder as she looked at me, she didn't even shrug away. "Is there a problem?"

"What are you doing, Sain?" Joclyn snarled, her voice little more than a hiss as she turned back to her father, his lips curling.

"I am sure the Chosen wish to see the power of their Queen!" Joclyn was frozen as Sain pulled away, yelling to the crowd who instantly erupted into cheers.

'What have I done?' The thought drifted from her so faintly that I wasn't sure if I had heard her, or if I was even meant to hear.

"What say you?" Sain goaded the crowd again, the cheers increasing as everyone pressed against the edge of the fountain, pressing against Wyn and Ryland who jumped up onto the edge of the fountain in an attempt to push them back. Poor Risha was nearly swallowed by the crowd.

"So, this is a mess," Wyn growled, letting sparks fly from her fingers as if it would control the crowd, the show of her magic only excited them more. "I say we get out of dodge and let Sain clean up this disaster."

"Nonsense. Sain wouldn't put Jos in a bad situation," Ryland's voice was calm as he stuck up for his friend, he seemed to be the only one interested in doing so.

'Yeah, I highly doubt that.' Joclyn's grumble was loud in my mind, her eyes searching mine as whatever fear had plagued her vanished and the wall in our connection faded to nothing. 'Promise me you will tackle him or something if anything goes wrong.'

'You have my word.' It was an easy promise to make, but it did not lessen my nerves about what was about to happen.

"I don't need the Black Water to see into Ilyan's life, for we are connected." Joclyn was confident, my back however was in knots, the tension becoming an iron band against my spine as her eyes dipped to black and Sain's smile spread.

The crowd waited, breaths held with a collective gasp as I stepped closer, jostling Wyn and Ryland to the side in order to reach her, to give her my magic and do whatever was needed to cause the water to flow.

The spark of her sight was moving through me, her magic swelling as her vision of some future began.

The water didn't so much as bubble. The rush of water

never came, instead it was only the mumbled questions of the crowd, Chosen and Skříteks alike looking from me to Joclyn as they waited for something to begin.

For something to happen.

"There is a beast inside the wall..." She began, her voice deep and monotone in sight, but the water did not bubble and the murmurs built into a wall of sound drowning out the sight as her words broke and caught in her throat again.

"Enough!" My command was a bark, even though my magic was carefully restrained, everyone reacting with a jerk as I pulled Joclyn back and into me.

The palm that had been burned by the Black Water pressed against her arm, her Drak magic reacting in a pull that flooded through me, showing me the sight in full detail. So much of it was the same as before, the five of us against the barrier, fighting a flood of Edmund's men that were coming so fast that we could barely keep up. Risha was falling to her knees in what I could only assume as death.

As quickly as the sight filled me, it left, washed away by the force of our magic as it collided, and as the water finally reacted to the Drak in her.

Instead of rising up in a tower of projected sight, however, it swarmed into the air and over us like a wave. Soaking all who stood on the side of the fountain and the first few rows of onlookers.

"This is bull." Wyn said as we all stood, soaking wet. The crowd was lost in laughter and shock, and Sain standing with a smile on his face.

4

JOCLYN

THE BIGGEST PROBLEM with living in an apocalypse is the lack of running water, and therefore a clear lack of washing machines, or showers, or even a steady drip from a faucet to drive you mad. Literally.

We could use magic and perhaps a careful combination of gravity and clean pipes to summon the occasional shower. For the most part, however, we all walked around in clothes in varying degrees of dirt and disarray, everything growing more grungy and worn until we could make another casual stop at an abandoned department store. It had been about a week since the last raid of that sort, which somehow made the whole fountain incident a blessing in disguise.

Or, it would have if I wasn't quite so pissed about what had happened.

I needed a shower, but I didn't need one that was quite so public or full of ridicule.

I was still pretty pissed about it. Okay maybe not pissed so much as really freakin' embarrassed.

"If you scowl much deeper you are going to look like a

five day old potato," Wyn threw a grungy towel at me before returning to wringing the water from her hair, letting dark strings of liquid snake over her hands and pool on the floor in a puddle that was more mud than water. As if we needed the reminder of how dirty we were, I didn't want to see how much more vile this towel was going to be after I was done with it.

"Good, I'm one step closer to my ultimate goal," I was trying to wring the water out of my shirt, which was proving to be a fool's errand. The thing was already full of holes; it's good that it was a dark color or I would have been participating in a one-woman wet t-shirt contest.

Gross.

"You want to look like an old potato?" Her forehead wrinkled underneath the damp strands of her hair, her dark eyes quirking in confusion.

"If it'll scare him off, sure," I jutted my chin toward where the men where drying off on the other side of the large medieval kitchen we always used for our meetings. The large dark underground room felt even more cold and drafty thanks to the fountain water.

The three of them were standing around one of the old fire pits, their bodies casting odd shadows over the grey stone walls thanks to the deep green flames someone had created.

Wimps. I was sure they were doing more than looking like apocalypse survivors who had created fire for the first time, but I didn't see any of it. My focus was digging into my father who was looking as confident and sniveling as ever. I wasn't sure how he accomplished the look so well, but even from this side of the room his nose had managed to upturn even more.

Which was probably why Ilyan looked about ready to

explode. Ryland stood between him and Sain like some kind of human shield. The imagery twisted my stomach.

Yes, Ry and I were in a weird place and while I didn't expect him to be standing up for my honor, watching him side with my father was a tad bit frustrating.

Okay, really freakin' frustrating.

"We should head over there," Risha announced as she came up behind us her arms full of rolled up maps and the box of stones we had been using as place holders. "I don't like the look on any of their faces."

The glance she gave me made it clear that I was included in that. I was already dragging my old potato scowl over there, wringing my hair out with one hand, and carrying a stack of gross towels with another.

"I understand your reasoning, Sain," Ilyan's voice had all the strength of a mini tornado behind it. "But you are not leading the charge on training the Chosen. They were not ready to see such things, you must clear these types of things --"

"Clear it with who?" Sain was so much calmer than Ilyan that his voice might as well have been ice with how it trailed down my spine like a snake. "You say I am not responsible for the training of the Chosen, but who is Ilyan? You? It seems you have stretched yourself too thin to be able to think clearly concerning the Chosen, or anything else for that matter."

Whether he meant to or not his eyes darted to me, the customized look of hatred that was made for me digging into my soul. Fire and fury rose up at the hate in his eyes and I dropped the towels, magic pricking at the hairs on the back on my neck as I went into a hate-fueled high alert.

"What is the anything else, Sain?" I said his name with too much malice, earning me a frustrated look from Ryland,

and quick pull back from Wyn, whose hands wrapped around my biceps as she pulled me into her. She was dry now thanks to the heat that was radiating off her skin.

Wish I had that trick.

'Don't let him goad you, my love. Or you will turn into an ugly old potato,' His voice was calm and didn't match the snarl on his face as he stepped between Sain and I, blocking him from view.

'Not funny.' I was in a full snarl now.

"I will appoint someone into that position who is capable of making unprejudiced decisions." Ilyan's voice was the low roar he always took on when taking on his role as King. Powerful. Strong. And enough warning to make me cringe. I knew what was coming, and I was trying not to look too smug about it.

Okay, I wasn't trying too hard. I could hear the words in Ilyan's mind before he spoke them, and Sain couldn't see me, so it didn't matter how much I was letting my pride show. Even Wyn was smiling and she couldn't hear the thoughts and frustrations that were rolling around in Ilyan's head. His tone was enough.

"Until then you are forbidden from any more public spectacles."

"Forbidden?" Sain stuttered over Ilyan, the single word sending his magic flaring through the room in a wave.

Ilyan stepped away from me, toward my father who was scowling so intently that his eyebrows might as well have fused together into one glorious unibrow. If unibrows could be glorious. It was a good look for him, made him look even more like an evil puppet.

"Yes forbidden." Ilyan's magic hit a high point and pooled into his words. Even with our connection I felt my magic tighten, my spine straighten, in a need to obey. The feeling was odd, especially when combined with the shadow of regret that washed over Ilyan. It might be a cool trick, but he certainly hated doing it. Wyn straightened and took one step away as if that would help her avoid whatever binding Ilyan was putting into his words.

"All training with the Chosen must be cleared with me, the queen, or with Risha. There is to be no more public spectacle, no lessons or training done without the permission of--"

"I am of the first! You can't be serious, my lord?" Sain interrupted with a hiss that was as green as his eyes. I thought the binding power in Ilyan's words was bad, the malice that drenched Sain's was making everything feel dangerous. Even my magic reacted with a spark and before I knew it, I was pushing myself passed Ilyan, coming face to face with my father and the malice riddled green on his eyes.

"We are. Things cannot be done now as they were a thousand years ago." I tried very hard to ignore the streak of pride that was bridging between Ilyan and I, but my lips twitched into a smile anyway. "The world is different. The world is falling apart because that little boy that you threw into the fire and showed all the magic in the world is currently trying to exterminate all of us. Surely you of all people can *see* how repeating the same action could cause trouble."

The danger dripped even deeper in his eyes, the look stretching into his jaw which was clenching so tightly it appeared to have its own pulse.

"You are young, my daughter, your power is weak. I see all. You do not know of our ways..."

"So you will teach the Chosen of *our* ways, but not your own daughter?" Yes, I was shrieking a tad bit more than was really 'queen-appropriate', which I would have been more worried about if Sain's dripping anger hadn't risen up to slap him upside the face.

He looked a bit slapped too. Even he was aware I had backed him into too much of a corner for him to talk his way out of it.

Ilyan's warm palm pressed against the wet and holey back of my shirt, his magic and pride sweltering through me as though the emotions were a furnace. Any other time it would soothe away my frustrations like the best deep tissue massage, but Sain had me so wound up it almost felt like he had pulled my pull cord.

"I am of the first. I know of this world and will teach all those who are ready to accept the truth of my magic." So much for being backed into a corner. My father had this special ability of using his pride like a spring board.

He was back up and fighting, and Ilyan's hand was there to hold me back or I would be in this fight like one of those head popping robots.

"You will teach no one without prior approval from the proper channels," Ilyan roared over the daggers we were throwing back and forth, although he didn't step between us like a human shield.

That was Wyn and Risha. Wyn was standing beside me as if she had turned into my own personal bodyguard. Risha was beside Ilyan, standing as his second, although she seemed a little lost as to who she should be protecting. Although not as lost as Ryland who was running his hands through his hair in that agitated way that always spelled trouble.

'Ryland.' I warned, luckily Ilyan had noticed and stepped toward Sain with a sigh that washed the tension out of the air, the madness fading from Ryland's eyes, even

if Sain looked about as apt to explode as he did a minute before.

"I do not wish to undermine your role as a first in our community." Ilyan began, his voice more diplomatic than the deep roll of frustration that I could feel bristling in his magic. "Your knowledge and your magic is valued in our community, but my wife, the queen, is correct. We cannot do things the way they have been done before or we risk a loop of history that will hurt our kind for generations more."

'Knowledge if you are deemed worthy of it.' Thank goodness for internal monologues, because I couldn't be as diplomatic as I needed to be when concerning my shower scum of a father.

I was already aware I should try harder, not that I cared. I straightened with a low sigh, earning myself a look from Wyn that was promptly followed by the eye roll I usually got when she caught me internalizing to Ilyan.

"I see no such loop of time. Teaching them this way is the right thing to do." His confidence was infuriating.

"I thought the sight was broken? How can you see if the sight is broken?" Wyn's accusation was like the candle of hope in a dark cavern, if the candle of hope was held by a ridiculous looking clown.

For the second time in the last few minutes Sain looked as though he had been slapped. What I wouldn't have given to let out one good laugh. I choked down the sound and earned myself a look for the fuming man.

"This is not the behavior of a queen, nor of a Drak, child."

"Enough, Sain." Ilyan boomed, Ryland flinched and Risha moved one small step toward Sain. The tiny action was a scream in my mind. Pretty sure that wasn't the way the second was supposed to be moving.

47

Ilyan's anger was roaring back to life. He had clearly noticed Risha's side step.

"I have chosen Joclyn, your daughter, as my queen. You have vowed to respect the role, and in turn her. Your disrespectful comments must stop. I will be speaking to you about your opinions, and the vile actions you connect to them. In respect for her, for I, and for the crown we wear I am commanding all of us that we all refrain from training, or demonstrating magic to the Chosen without permission, and without orders. We will be deciding on a course of action for training the children, but for now the order is to limit any magical demonstrations of that size."

I doubt any of us could have fought against the command if we wanted to. Wyn, Ryland and Risha nodded in acceptance. Sain, however, looked likely to explode, his fists trembling against the tattered fabric of the suit he wore. I didn't want to know where he had dug that thing up. Even though it had been drenched with fountain water it still looked vile.

"Do not punish the powers of the Drak simply because the Queen failed to demonstrate a simple skill."

Ilyan was tall, easily standing a full head above me on any given day. Somehow he managed to grow a few extra inches right then, everything about him straightening as he stepped toward Sain, towering over the now quivering man. First of his kind or not, I think he lost a few feet of both height and ego right then.

"I am punishing you for putting the Chosen and the Queen in a place that can only lead to injury for our kingdom." Ilyan paused, although it was clear he wasn't giving my father a chance to counter. Sain's pride didn't fade, but he didn't step back either.

Well, he didn't. Risha took one large step toward Ilyan, her eyes downcast.

"I am punishing you for disrespecting the Queen in an act of both verbal and magical depravity. You should be glad it is not worse. You're dismissed." Ilyan was final, and this time Sain flinched, his jaw working its way opened as Ilyan stepped away, Risha following behind him like an apologetic dog. Made sense given what I had witnessed. Second-in-command's weren't supposed to have momentary lapses in commitment.

'They aren't.'

Yeah, I didn't want to be on the other side of the frustrated temper. The roar in his voice was like a tiger ready to rip limbs.

"What do you mean I am dismissed, Ilyan? We have a meeting..." The begging apology that I had hoped to see before this had officially made its appearance, although a bit too late and a bit too forced. He was looking like the girls in high school when the guy said no to their big elaborate ask to homecoming.

He made to take off after Ilyan, and was moving toward the table where Risha had deposited the rolls of maps, but I took one quick step before him, blocking his path.

"And you are no longer included." Harsh? Sure. But he deserved it.

I kept my shoulders as straight as I could as I faced him, grateful that Wyn had kept herself glued to my side like she was my own second.

I was pretty sure that Queens didn't get seconds or bodyguards, but if we did Wyn was the best second I could ask for. If her glares didn't burn you to death, her magic would.

Wait. What was I talking about *we*? I guess I had enrolled myself in some secret Queen club now.

"I suggest you go back to your quarters for a time, Father. Perhaps we can get together later, talk about 'our kind'." I sounded like my mother, which hurt for multiple reasons. If I had to be the responsible one in this situation I might as well embrace the role to its fullest extent.

"I highly doubt you will be ready for that any time soon, Joclyn." Not that it did any good, his ego had made a grand return.

"Then I doubt you will be ready to join us anytime soon. We have our own little club here, no snivelers allowed." Wyn's sass poured out of her with a dainty little wave of her hand and any chance of being responsible left as one loud laugh escaped from me before I was able to restrain it.

"Wyn!" Ilyan boomed from where he was unfurling maps, the single word reducing her to giggles as she threw her arm around my shoulder, giving Sain a wink through her chuckle.

"I would hate for you to make a mistake here, Sain," She continued, before pulling me toward Ilyan and the meeting, leaving the poor man to embrace another word slap. Except this time I could have sworn he looked scared.

And not the usual pissed that someone isn't treating him like a god scared. Like truly, there is a monster standing behind us, scared.

By the time I had twisted in Wyn's somewhat forceful guide toward the meeting he had turned away, storming out of the hall with the bang of the wood door behind him. Leaving both Ryland and I to stand confused in his wake.

"What in the world was that about, Wyn?" Ry asked as he jogged up in front of us, pulling us to a stop a few steps before the table.

I peaked my eyebrow at her, Ryland had taken the question right out of my mouth.

"Do you have some kind of superpower? I can't get him to even blink at me, and he hates me. You chased him away..."

"Not that." Ry snapped, his eyes darting away as he pulled at his hair again. We had officially stepped into dangerous territory. I could feel both magic and madness battle against each other at the look in his eyes, but I refused to step away. We couldn't keep moving forward if I was always taking one step back.

'You alright, my love?' His voice was calm in my head, even though he was only a few feet from us and could intercede.

'Completely. It's just Ry.' And his crazies, but I wasn't going to admit that last part out loud, well out-mind. *'He's alright too. We've got this.'*

"Why did you talk to him like that?" Ryland's eyes were a little shaky when they pulled back to me, yes me. Because he was no longer looking at Wyn.

"Do we need to go over this again? I know he protected you, Ry, but I have yet to see that."

"That doesn't mean that he should get punished..."

"He told every Chosen that we have rescued, that I have healed, that I disrespect him and used some kind of magical prowess to become queen." Repeating the cliffs notes of the conversation was as stabby and painful as the real thing.

"He was upset..."

"That doesn't make it okay," didn't make the stabbing pain in my chest go away either. "Look, Ry, I'm not writing him off, but until he starts acting like he's one of us and not above us," read: above me, "we can't have him included in everything."

"But we need him for this mission." We had reached the table now, the large maps that we had been carefully cultivating over the last week already laid out. "We need him to see when we are supposed to leave."

"I think I have seen that," I said calmly, earning myself a shocked glance from everyone but Ilyan who was still placing pebbles in the ink circles that were littered in the streets on the north end of the wall.

"Just today, when fighting Wyn and again by the fountain. I saw the mission, I know what's going to happen. I will be able to see anything that's headed our way when we are there too. Don't worry. We will be fine without him."

I was confident. Sure. And lying a little bit. Ilyan was aware of that, the tiny twist of a smile clear even though his focus was still on the map.

'I should tell them about the battle.'

'We need to look again, just to be sure.' I was trying not to bristle at that. I wanted him to trust my sights as much as I did. But right then I wasn't super sure how much I was trusting them.

The sight I had seen by the fountain had showed the courtyard we had been planning this mission in at least three times, each time a different scenario. Each time a different group of people doing a variety of things.

But it was our group, and this thing that we had been planning that had pulled at me so abruptly. With Edmund's men tearing through the barrier, right toward us and the blood soaked world.

'There are too many inconsistencies.' I hated admitting it if only because it meant that there might be some truth to what my irritating father was saying.

About broken sights. Scratch that, *my* broken sights.

'I know your sights are true, my darling. They will know

again, soon.' His confidences whispered into my mind, even though his focus was on arranging the scale models that Risha had made out clay.

That's what it all came down to. He, Wyn, and probably even Dramin, they wouldn't question. But Risha and Ryland would. Even I had seen her step away.

I moved her little clay figure closer to the one of my father, wishing that I could stomp him out of existence.

Sometimes I wondered where the girl found time. I was the Drak, we don't sleep, and I doubt I could find the time to make clay figures. Especially anything as intricate at these. Sain's tattered clay jeans were perfect. I would have to guess that she was getting as much, or as little, sleep as I was.

"Joclyn will be able to take on any additional role that we expected of Sain. Her magic is strong and ready."

"Even if it's just for another shower, it'll be the best shower of your life, and I'll make it warm this time." Not even Wyn laughed at that one. The girl twisted her lips into an obligatory grin and picked at one of the rocks that denoted what we thought was a Vilỳ nest.

It was hard to tell where they were, and even with Wyn and my crazy magic working overtime we hadn't been able to track their movements.

Which was partially why Sain being on this trip was important. A different kind of early alert system.

"The only shower I want is on the other side of this wall, so this better work," Wyn mumbled, still picking at the rock with the chipped end of her nail.

"You might get just that," Ilyan said as he traced his finger through the road and toward the edge of the barrier, to the exact spot we had planned to break a few days ago, and the exact courtyard I had seen in so many sights today.

Nothing else about the sights had been the same except

that courtyard, well and Wyn's shirt, although without the cape I am not sure it counted.

"Remember," Ilyan continued, pulling me from my recall, and my multiplying confusion. "We need to control the break enough to get us out and keep the Vilỳ in. We can't unleash those things on the world. And Edmund's men are getting in somehow, so that means we should be able to get out."

"Does that mean that operation pop Edmund's Zit is a go?" Wyn's laugh was trouble.

"I think it best if we leave now considering what this day has already set for us," Ilyan cut in, stoically ignoring the perfectly good suggestion of a name for the dome.

'We aren't calling it that,' I had barely been able to control the smile at Wyn's question before, now I was doomed.

'Yes, we are, I am converting everyone one at a time.'

'Stalled at Wyn, did you?'

I was caught between real and false shock, my jaw sagging in playful aghast... that Ilyan thoroughly ignored.

"Gather any supplies you need and meet at the exit point."

"I'll get my cloak," Wyn said with a wink before skipping away, out of the door that led away from her room. For Wyn, gathering supplies still meant to take one last check on Thom.

Risha said nothing before walking away, Ryland giving one last look at me before turning to his brother, his shoulder taut and straight in the way that always meant business for him.

"Are you sure this is wise?"

"I have seen this..."

"I don't want us to get stuck in a bad situation," Ryland cut me off, not even looking at me as he stared at his brother, at the King who cleaned the maps with a wave of his hand, his eyes not looking at any of us.

"I believe our Queen was trying to tell you something."

Suddenly, I hated the title more than I ever had. I hated being stood up for. I hated the look in Ryland's eyes and everything that was hovering over the table between us. And I didn't just mean the map pieces.

My confidence and power might as well have melted away right then.

"It will be fine Ryland. Sain will be fine." I didn't know what I was saying. I didn't know which was the lie, or if both of them were, but it didn't matter.

Ryland's eyes narrowed in warning before he walked away without another word, just as defiantly as Sain had. Even though I tried to ignore it, it hurt just as much. The door slammed behind him and I jumped, the tiny clay figure of Sain that I held smashing between my fingers.

5

SAIN

"You're late, Sain."

Ovailia's tone was dripping with as much false flattery and honey as the last time I saw her, her lips were turned up into the slightest of smiles, her stance casual as she leaned against the grimy wall of the building we usually met beside. Leather glimmered in the faint red light of the dome, the perfectly tailored jacket and boots looking too new. She had clearly rescued them from the expensive department store across the street before our meeting.

She was beautiful, and my heart and magic raced into the marathon that I usually found myself battling when I was around her. The need of her would have been so much stronger if the hatred and power wasn't ruling her eyes, the emotions as dark as the leather in both shoes and jacket.

It wasn't the first time I had to remind myself that I did not need her.

That she was better off dead.

"It took some time to get away." My voice shook and rattled as I approached at a hobble, purposefully letting my left foot drag as I always did when I was around her, fueling the image of the weak pathetic worm they had created.

The shake in my voice, however, was from the pure rancid hatred that was pulsing through my veins. I wasn't late because it was hard to get away. I was late because I had chosen to go destroy a hidden corner of the city and vent my frustrations there, instead of on her.

I may not have laid buildings to waste, but a few hundred Vilÿs were still bleeding over the darkened alley streets, their mutilated bodies inching closer to death. Seeing as I couldn't destroy Ilyan and his vulgar ego, it was the next best thing.

For now.

I wasn't going to be able to allow Ilyan and my bastard child to treat me like that much longer. I, one of the first, deserved more than that.

So much more.

"Next time, perhaps you can take more control of Ilyan and his vermin and not leave me waiting." Ovailia pulled me from my quickening heart and anger with a snap, some of the lust in her tone fading as she tapped her nails against her arm, the long red talons looking even more blood soaked in this light.

"You don't seem to have been idle in waiting." A bit of the warble in my voice left as I gestured to the jacket and boots, my magic heating back into its own lustful tango at seeing how high up her thigh they journeyed.

Anger be damned, leave it to Ovailia to distract me with other things.

I swallowed. She noticed and her smile stretched, the warmth of her magic twisting through the air in such a way I was sure I was meant to feel it.

"You like the boots, Sain?" Power dripped from her voice, the strength of her ripping through the marathon.

It was getting harder to find the vulnerability in her. I had spent so many years watching her cower under those above her. Ilyan. Edmund. Myself. But somehow over the last hundred years, the years that I had spent running with Thom, beguiled by a mortal and a false memory, she had found a strength that I may not have expected of her otherwise.

Beautiful. Just like the boots.

"I do."

"Good. Take it all in, because if you are late again I will use them to make sure you forget the last hundred years, as well as any memory of my legs!" She snapped, this time with a hard palm slapped across my jaw and I jerked into the cower that I had done for so many centuries that it was becoming more normal to me than I would like to acknowledge.

Edmund. Ilyan. And now Ovailia. I hadn't wanted to add her to the list.

Soon. They would all be under me again, soon.

"Ovi... Ovailia," I corrected as I moved to stand, rubbing my jaw as I faced her. "I cannot always leave on a moment's notice, Ilyan was with me. Ilyan was watching."

My voice was mangled from the ache in my jaw, my magic pushing through it as I healed the bone, although there wasn't much there to heal. She may have strength in her eyes but she still hit like a girl.

"Ilyan is always watching, and if you can't escape my brother and his starry-eyed child bride than perhaps you are no good to us. Perhaps you are no good to me."

Even I could tell that her threat was hollow. Harsh words, a sly smile, yet the scent of her magic swelled, pressing against me as if in reminder of what I could have. What I had. I no longer wished that of her, but it didn't stop me from playing this lustful tango with her.

"No, Ovi. I can help. I am helping. Please don't end me..." Not that I would allow such a thing to happen.

"And yet, you have failed to give us any information on the location of Ilyan's camp." She was now inspecting the long blood soaked color of her nails, her focus drifting between me and the nails as I cowered. Shoulders hunched, magic shaking against my spine.

"I have told you, Ilyan has bound us all. I cannot even speak of the--" Anything I was about to say was swallowed by Ilyan's magic as the bind he had placed on us all activated. My head screamed with the sound of a foghorn, wiping any and all thought of the location from my mind, my throat constricted, taking all ability to speak with it.

I sounded like a drowning cat, screeching and howling as I was.

Ovailia burst into laughter, the sound drenched with malice as she stepped away from the wall, rising to her full height as she towered over me. Her hair swung through the dark at the moment, bathing the air in the scent of her. The aroma of lust.

The cat drowned into silence as my magic attempted to betray me, the emotion helped along by her long nails tripping over the tattered seams of the suit as she stepped behind me.

"You have found ways around Ilyan's binding before, I believe you can do the same this time. Find a way, Sain," She spoke the last words into my ear, whispering gently as she picked at the tattered edge of the collar, the collar I had spent a bit too much time making as disarrayed as it was.

People were much more likely to follow someone they

could see themselves in. And we were all a little tattered right now.

"It may not be possible this time, Ovailia. I cannot write the location down. I cannot think beyond the alarm in my head when I even try to hint at the location." Even getting that close opened up into an irritating buzzing and I cringed, my face screwing up in an agony as Ovailia leaned closer to me, her fingers tiptoed across my shoulder now, down my arm. "I cannot tell you."

Ilyan had gone above his usual bindings this time, the painful alarm system extreme for even his paranoia. He assumed that he would be double crossed. Which while true, was certainly working to my benefit. I could break that bind without much effort, but it gave me an excellent excuse to keep the information from her. Or rather, from her father. I doubt Ovailia could do much on her own.

Not that I didn't need her to find Ilyan and his camp, but I had a few cards to play before that happened. Besides, the more I made her work for it, the more entertaining it was for me.

Dangle the mouse before the beautiful feline.

"I am sure you can find a way, Sain," She was pressed against me now, the traveling nails having snaked all the way down my arm to tap gently against the back of my hand. Between the touch and the pressure of her magic it was taking far too much self-control to keep myself away from her.

"Can you do this for me, Sain?" Her voice was a low moan that I hadn't heard in years and I almost lost it.

I could shiver. I could groan. I could grab her and press her against the wall and give myself away. So instead I moaned in fear instead of pleasure, cowered, and shimmied away from her, keeping my focus on the shiny leather toes of her boots, one of which was scuffed.

"I can, I know I can." It wasn't a lie.

"Wonderful, we will need the location soon." Perhaps, I have been too hasty in my promise. "To prepare for what is coming."

"For what is coming?" Dread rippled from my toes to the crown of my head. They couldn't be ready to send their pitiful army through the wall yet, could they? I had seen the attack as Joclyn had, but I was sure we had more time. A few days at the least.

"I am surprised you have not seen what is about to happen, Sain. I would tell you if I wasn't so disappointed in you." Oh, I had seen it, but I cowered and stared at my shoes all the same, the mud I had caked on earlier having washed off thanks to Joclyn's foolish attempt at sight at the fountain.

I hadn't even had to block her visions, she had messed that one up all on her own, the untrained imposter.

"That is unless you have something new that you are dying to share? Some little tidbit of those bastard children that Joclyn has healed rising up against me? I know you don't want them to rise up against me."

She paused, her lips twisting into question as she circled closer, so close that I could smell the scent of the soap she had used that morning. The magic of the sandalwood was still clinging to her skin. I could stand here and breath her in all day, and not just because it masked the smell of rotten death that filled Prague outside of Ilyan's perfect little fortress.

Death was not a smell I normally minded. The aroma of blood, of life and magic as it drifted into the air could be relaxing at times.

But this was the stench of death left too long, and it was more rot than loss.

"I can hardly believe that you haven't seen anything at all this last month. I would hate to have to pull it out of you." The calm question was gone, replaced by malicious dread as she stepped closer still, the smell of her so strong that it was making it hard to think.

Perhaps that was her plan.

There was plenty I could tell her, but not much that I was ready to give up. This was a careful game I was playing, and it was becoming a dangerous one if Ovailia was growing impatient.

I would have to be careful with this.

"There is one thing," I spoke as reluctantly as I could, stepping back and forcing my muscles to tense, my eyes dropping to the ground in a false fear that she had no chance to see through. If she hadn't seen through it in a millennium there was no hope for her now.

"Joclyn has been showing signs of weakness." I heaved an exasperated sigh, wrinkling my brow in worry, whereas Ovailia perked up, the red in her eyes flashing like a light.

"Weakness? My, my Sain, you have been holding back." Ovailia's voice dripped with eagerness as she stepped back to me.

Instead of the towering threat that loomed through the shadow of the building, however, her face was soft, her hand gentle as it lifted to wipe away the faded memory of a bruise that was trying to grow on my jaw. The tips of her fingers lifted, forcing me to look at her, and I found myself challenged by her for the third time.

She was certainly making things difficult.

Everything about her was fire. The air around her rippled, her eyes blazed, and some part of her fell away.

I would love to say that I had a hand in this grooming skill she had mastered, but I had seen that look before on another. I couldn't take all the credit.

Wyn had helped to create this beauty too, thousands of years before. I could see the resemblance of the whore clear in Ovailia's eyes, I wonder if Wyn had seen it yet now that she had regained her memories.

"Tell me, is it weakness in sight, or is the weakness in her power?" It was now that I hesitated. What to tell her? The answer I gave could impact the next few steps I would have to take. I did not have time to see what repercussions either would lead to. I would have to take what would come.

"It is her sight. She cannot call the power to her as it once was." I was careful to keep the pride out of my voice. "Today she was not able to call sight at all."

It was a bit of an exaggeration, but Ovailia need never know that. She and her father wanted information, and information I would deliver. If they chose to interpret the information I gave as factual. that was a problem only for them.

To me, everything was still going to plan.

"Is this falter part of your hand, Sain?" Lustful need, or the illusion of it, shone from Ovailia's eyes as her hand finally left my chin to trace over my jaw and down my neck. The tips of her fingers played with the hair there, her nails tracing over the skin, pricking against my flesh with enough pressure that the touch became more of a threat than an allure.

"Are you destroying your daughter's mind?" Her voice was as harsh as her touch, the point of her nails returning to her side, and tapping against the building.

"I could never do such thing." It was hard to maintain the weakness in my voice, to keep the desire from my eyes.

She was watching me too closely to let that show. "It destroyed me to watch you and Cail hurt her so. My daughter... You know my magic does not have the capability, even if I wanted to do such a thing. And I wouldn't. She is my daughter, Ovi."

My spine straightened as Ovailia laughed, the sound nothing but ridicule as it bounced off the stone wall and called to the little rats that lay hidden through the city. I could already hear the faint call of the beasts as they rushed toward us, ready to meet their end with only a word. Not that it would happen, they would keep their distance once they saw the two of us.

"Don't take me for a fool, Sain," Ovailia said, "You can't expect me to think that you love the girl. You hate children. You hate things you cannot control. And I know for a fact that this girl will fight any control you try to place her under."

She was right of course. The value of keeping people around me was in my ability to use them. I had been able to do that to everyone, Joclyn included.

That information was not for Ovailia, however. Neither was my part in my daughter's sudden struggles with her magic.

"She has wanted a father for her entire life, you clearly do not know the girl as much as you would think."

I leaned into Ovailia, pressing her against the building as she inhaled. Shock washed over her face as it drenched my stomach. I was a fool to be so brazen, but she didn't seem to mind, her magic arched through the air and pressed against mine as she leaned toward me. Moving closer.

The shock faded as her magic did, her eyes hardening as she pushed away the emotion.

"If you have such an adoring daughter, I am sure you

would love to help us in another way." Ice slithered up my spine with the way her focus had hardened, the way she leaned into me.

"Wh- what are you asking?" I didn't force the stutter that time. It came naturally, the lusty need I felt for her a minute ago melting into nothing.

Any answer she could give me would be unwelcome. Any answer was bound to affect my current trajectory in some unwanted way.

"Bring her doubt," She smiled, and by some miracle the tension that had wound through my back relaxed. "She was destined to kill my father, and she failed. In magic, in sight. That must be quite a blow. So, bring her doubt. Doubt of her ability. Of her place. Of my brother's foolish love for her. Rip her apart in other ways. Cripple her as my father could not."

I didn't restrain the smile, although I chose not to bring attention to her acknowledgement of her father's failure, and of my assumed success. And succeed I would. After what Ilyan had done to me, after his disregard and humiliation against my place in his kingdom there was only one course of action. I had never had a need for him, after all.

Ovailia and I were in agreement of what needed to happen for the first time in centuries.

"As you will, my lady." I spoke carefully, feeding her ego as I used the title that she had lusted after for so long. The title I would give her in the darkest of nights when we were together.

I could never be sure, but the answering smile she gave me then seemed too genuine for the game we were playing, for the game that was pulling her right into my hands.

6

JOCLYN

"THOSE ARE AUTUMN LEAVES. I can see them dance in the breeze, ready to twirl to the ground before winter."

"Dancing leaves, twirling to the ground. Geeze, Jos. I think I might have rubbed off on you too much."

"You are trying not to see them, Wyn."

I was so close to the barrier that my breath kept fogging over the red barrier. Each breath sent angry ripples of magic dashing over the surface like lightning, just as it would if we were to touch the dratted thing.

I had been dumb enough to do that in the first week, but would have to have officially lost my mind to do it again. One spine twisting magical attack was enough.

Keeping the space of a breath between me and the sparking wall, I leaned as close as I could. Even though you couldn't see the outside world any clearer no matter how close you got.

"Yep, totally autumn leaves. I'm ninety percent sure."

"And I'm ninety percent sure it's just you smudging your nose against a red window. Those may not even be trees, and those leaves sure as heck aren't dancing. Writhing to their death maybe," Wyn was adamant that I was wrong, but she was also standing as close to the barrier as I was, eyes squinting as we tried to see through it.

Ilyan had said there was some farmland past here, and in the distance a tiny little village surrounded by fields and grazing cattle. I was sure I had seen a cow during one of our visits here, although with how the wall distorted everything this close to where it met with the ground I could be looking at a dinosaur resurrected from the dead and partially consumed by zombies.

Anything could happen. Who knew what was going on over there. We could see the planes that were always circling overhead clear as day. But zombie cows? That was a mystery.

"It's probably not even autumn, Jos," Wyn took a step back and shook her head to clear the red light from her eyes, as if dislodging the wash of red was possible this close to the barrier.

Everything was so saturated with red it looked as though it was soaked with blood. Blood drenched stones, the sides of the buildings, even the dying trees and grass were bathed with red. Everything, including us, just like in the sight. That was enough to freak anyone out, but we were all sweating so much that bright red drops of water were dripping over faces and arms and pooling against the backs of shirts like blood. It was like being stuck in a slasher flick.

Creepy.

"It could be autumn by now. The trees had begun to change before everything happened," Risha provided from where her and Ryland were setting up a weird makeshift barrier on the other side of the tiny courtyard. "They could have changed that much in a month."

"Six weeks," Ilyan corrected, flicking his fingers and letting his magic do the heavy lifting as he brought a massive boulder over to where the others were, adding to the multiplying barricade. He was too nonchalant about all of it, boulder, time frame, impending attack.

Well, he seemed that way. His heart rate was elevated and I was sure if I put my palm flat against his back his muscles would be tied in tight little knots.

He got a look from me anyway. "That isn't helping."

I didn't like the reminder of how long we had been trapped here as much as anyone else. Everyone's face fell in a dejected concern, the boulder Risha had been lugging over to the pile dropping to the ground with a whack. Thankfully, I had a shield around us that reflected sound a bit. I would really like to not put that to the test however. We were going to be creating a lot more noise in a few minutes, the less Vilỳs we attracted before we attempted to pop this bubble, the better.

Hopefully, I could focus enough to create a small hole, get a few of us out, and not the entire army of deranged Vilỳ. Not that I could control what was about to go down. There wasn't exactly a way to practice.

"Six weeks and we haven't been able to pop the barrier yet..." Ryland began, trying to arrange Ilyan's boulder on top of the teetering pile of rubbish that they were building.

"I still prefer Joclyn's suggestion of 'Edmund's Zit'. It sounds much more refined." Wyn interrupted with a grin and a pop of her hip, throwing a twisted piece of metal onto the pile, the thing looked like it had been a chair in a past life.

"Refined things don't normally seep puss, Wynifred," Ilyan wasn't in the mood for joking, his face and voice were a little too stern considering we were talking about puss.

"Ew." Ryland popped up from behind the tiny wall of rubble they were building to stare at us, curls bouncing as his face wrinkled together. "Does that make us the puss? Because I don't want to be puss."

"I am officially resigning my stand of calling the barrier Edmund's Zit." The trees were forgotten, my stomach was now doing its own circus act, complete with twists and turns and all sorts of 'threatening to turn our contents inside out' flippies.

Zits were all fun and games until someone brought up the puss.

"You are the only puss among us, Ry." Wyn smiled broadly and stepped out of the leather heels she had picked up in some clothing store last week. The things were far nicer than anything I had seen her wear before, and although they looked nice, they were something I was more likely to see on Ovailia than Wyn.

Which I had told her.

Which she was still definitely fighting me on as she placed her bare foot against the ground, fixing me with an upturned scowl as she flashed the shoes at me like she was a foot model. I rolled my eyes at her. Those things were ridiculous and not meant for fighting.

Not that we were here for that, at least to their knowledge.

The images from the sight were still pounding on the back of my mind, the red tinted world doing nothing to help me banish the bright red blood from my mind.

'We will know soon about the sight. And we will be ready either way,' Ilyan soothed, his magic wrapping around my heart. *'It could be any number of things, my love. Perhaps it is not even this day.'*

I knew he meant well, but it wasn't helping. One look at Risha was all I needed to know that this was the time, and the place. I had seen her fall to her knees, seen the blood spill over the blue patterned shirt as her eyes went blank. It was the same shirt, the same high ponytail she usually wore when we were out in the city. It was the same.

You don't get images like that out of your head.

'And yes, I know that we all have limited wardrobes,' I amended my thought, I knew full well that Ilyan was listening. *'It's today.'*

'Your sight is correct, Joclyn. I know this. This fight will be like any other. We will face that truth and take whatever repercussions come after.' There Ilyan went with his ultimate positivity, it was a tad bit infectious.

'You mean confront Sain when we kick these guys butts and I am right. Again.'

His magic swelled joyfully as he placed one final boulder on top of the pile, everyone stepping away as Wyn cracked her knuckles like she was getting ready to play baseball, and not melt rocks into a wicked protective wall.

"Lift your feet if you want to keep them," She said with a smile, the ground heating even before she had finished giving her warning.

Our conversation was cut off as the fire that was snaking over the cobbles spiked, and as one we all lifted ourselves into the air, hair and clothes whipping around as magic and wind supported us in the air and kept us away from the burning ground.

It was like that game you play as a kid when the floor is lava. Except Wyn's lava floor could burn your legs down to stubble.

Between the heat of Wyn's magic, and the movement of magical air, the boiling temperature of being this close to the barrier was reaching a breaking point. The sweat that was pooling around the back of my neck, and dripping over my skin, picked up in earnest.

Water rolled over my skin, the hot fluid frightening as Wyn's magic flooded into the pile of rubbish. The rock heated and boiled, the solid stone beginning to melt and roll over the rubble and garbage that made of up our pile, turning it all into a solid form of lava. Even the mangled chair that had added began to glow, the wrought iron legs twisting over the surface of bubbling stone as though it was building a cage.

Given the frightening reflection of fire in Wyn's dark eyes, and the twisted smile that was covering her features I would have to guess that that was exactly what she was doing.

She looked like an evil villain. Creepy.

The more her smile spread, the more the air heated until it felt as if it was boiling against my skin, the ember glow of Wyn's magic pulsing even more into the air. I would be worried I was about to be boiled alive if I wasn't so amazed with the work of art that she was creating.

"Jeeze Wyn, do you always try to melt the people around you when you use your magic?" Ryland asked, his hair was so soaked with sweat that it was straining over his face as though he had dunked his head in swamp water.

It wasn't a good look and made me thankful that my hair was braided, although I was sure the braid had melted and glued itself to the back of my neck.

"You don't want to see what happens when I try to melt the people around me." Wyn's smile was swallowing her whole now, her eyes shimmering with as much flame as the barrier she created.

"Remind me never to get on your bad side." Ryland returned, his voice shaking as he twitched, the motion slight, but still enough that everyone knew what was going on.

'Darn it. Do you think he's close?' I asked the question, but I was already trying to spread my magic out in search of the bastard that had messed with Ryland and I enough to drive us into insanity.

Ryland may have a good hold on his magic nowadays, but it had only been a month since his last outburst. Bringing him this close to the barrier in the first place had been a bit of a gamble. It didn't help that my normally super powerful ability to track and scan was rendered useless from Edmund's red wall. Just like the trees, I couldn't get a clear enough picture to know if it was Edmund who has getting too close or a particularly dapper circus bear.

'There is no way to know, we have to keep working.' Ilyan was giving the wall some serious side-eye as he tried to see through it himself. I hated how useless the wall made everything.

Ilyan and I were not the only ones who had caught Ryland's slight jerk. Risha soared to his side in her attempt at support, her hand soft against his forearm.

"I will have to agree with that," Risha said, even though her focus was only on Ryland. "You are freaky, Wyn."

"Thank you." I wasn't even sure Wyn had witnessed the exchange, her focus was still on the barricade, the flames and molten pile of scary fading into something that appeared to be more artistic than an army base for 'if this plan goes so bad we might die'.

She had effectively molded the rocks and rubbish into a large igloo shape that they could all hide in, save a tiny door opposite Edmund's barrier the only other opening was a tiny slit like you would give a password through to get into a secret bar, or that you would push gun barrels through in a war.

Too bad this wasn't a password type situation.

'I suddenly have a bad feeling about this plan,' I tried to keep the moan out of my voice, something that wasn't working well seeing as a tense knot had decided to migrate to my spine.

"And we are clear," Wyn announced, everyone touching down seconds later, the hot wind boiling down to a warm and uncomfortable breeze as the wind dissipated into nothing.

I took one big cleansing breath of the not-quite-boiling air and stepped toward the red wall of Edmund's dome, my magic buzzing in my veins as if it knew what I was about to do.

'Your sight has brought us this far. It will continue to guide us in the right direction.'

'It also showed Risha dying in a flash of red light.' I interrupted, giving him a look as he came up behind me and held my mug out to me.

"What you saw with Sain this morning at the fountain was different than what Sain saw. It was different than what we had seen before. You have seen many possibilities, all of which could be true. We will take it as it comes." He spoke low enough that I was sure he was trying to stop us from being heard. Thank goodness Ryland and Risha were too wrapped up in each other at the moment. "You saw this moment, you saw this plan. That was different. I wouldn't trust anything that happens with Sain."

"I don't trust anything that even mentions his name." I may have been harsh, but I didn't care. I was too focused on refilling my mug at that point in time, something that I might be doing too vigorously considering that nerves and frustration were taking a siesta through my nervous system.

'I am more worried about what would happen if nothing happens?' I continued where no one could hear.

'It wouldn't be the first time a sight didn't happen. It wouldn't be the first time yours did, and his didn't either.' I shook my head at Ilyan's response, keeping the motion small enough that no one else would notice.

"Let's hope it's the no death version that wins out.' I let out a great heaving sigh which pulled the attention from Wyn who was bounding over to us, a giant smile on her face.

"Alrighty, let's pop this zit. Let Edmund eat the puss." Wyn had chosen the exact wrong time to make her announcement, and the water that I had taken a giant, hopefully relieving sip from, turned into a bomb in my mouth.

Black Water went down the wrong pipe, tried to migrate up my nose and left me sputtering and trying very hard not to spit all over everyone. All of this, while I made a sound that was more fitting coming from one of those screaming goats.

We didn't need to add black water burns and sight to our list of happenings in this little excursion. Of course, that now left me choking, Ilyan patting my back as everyone else took one large conspicuous step away.

Good. Because I was pretty sure black water was dripping from my nose. Cute.

"Thanks, Wyn," I choked, the goat sound continuing to blast from me and send her into a fit of giggles.

"Always best to start epic battles off on a high note, and seeing as we don't have any Slovokia around," she wiggled her eyebrows, but no one responded.

Instead, Ryland and Risha rolled their eyes in some weird tandem eyebrow dance and stepped into the dome Wyn had made.

"They don't know what they are missing," Wyn said with

a sigh and followed them in, calling behind her about letting us know when she needed to save our butts.

That time, it was Ilyan's turn to sigh and run his hands through his hair, or rather over the messy braid I had given him that morning. I really needed to get better at that.

"Let's get this over with, shall we?" I asked, placing the mug on the ground before stepping to the barrier and trying to ignore the three sets of eyes that were now staring at me from Wyn's peep hole.

And please don't let anyone die.

"I won't let that happen, my love," Ilyan whispered, stepping behind me the same as I had seen in the sight. His arms wrapped around my waist the same as they do each morning when he pulls me into him, his fingers lifting my shirt enough that the soft pads of his touch made contact with my skin.

Fire ran through my veins at the contact, my magic pooling under my skin, ready to break through the flimsy barrier and find him.

"I will protect you and all of my people." The deep rumble of his king voice vibrated in my ear before he leaned down, his lips moving closer to my mark, closer to the touch that would start all this.

Having his hands against my skin was sending my magic into a flurry, but that was only the pre-show to what was about to happen.

His breath was hot against my neck, his lips soft as they fluttered against my neck, shifting closer to my mark. I gasped when his touch made contact, when our magic went into a wave of energy that might as well have been a tsunami. The power washed over me, ready to escape, ready to work.

Everything was as it was in sight. The only question was, what was going to happen now?

I couldn't stand here forever and second guess, I had to act. So much for never touching the barrier again. With power and fire ruling my veins, I smashed the palms of my hands into the barrier, ready for the barrier to break and the world beyond to shine over us, autumn leaves and all.

Instead, the power I shot into the dome shot right back into my hands, combined with the power that normally ran through the barrier to keep us away. The warming comfort of our combined magic turned into a firestorm, everything burning and ripping and pulling so hard that it felt as if my bones were going to shoot out of my body in little splinters.

My scream ripped through the air as I tried to push my magic into the barrier, as I tried to escape the pain and redirect the magic somewhere, anywhere. Nothing was working, and it wasn't like before, I could no longer see a path for my magic to travel and destroy it.

Ilyan wasn't as affected as I. With a swipe, he shoved my hands away from the wall and toward the ground where they erupted with a blast that sent gravel, dirt, and former cobbles into the air around us, and buried us five feet down into what was once a road.

Dust and dirt swirled around us from the blast, the hard edge of stone and who knows what else cutting into the exposed skin on my arms and face. My magic buzzed as it raced to find and heal the cuts and broken skin, I wasn't sure there was anything, but I was still burning from whatever had happened. Thankfully, Ilyan was there to support me because my legs were suddenly unwilling to do the job.

Well, that didn't work. Even in my head I sounded exhausted, I didn't want to know how I was going to look coming out of this.

"Perhaps it did, just not in the way that was expected." Ilyan's eyes bored into the red wall that was poking through the bits of earth I had torn away.

The barrier extended far below the ground. That knowledge was nothing new, however, we had tried to burrow our way out, week one. The long crack that was rippling through the dirt, however, was new. The deep brown of the earth behind it was nearly forgotten.

The crack ran through the dirt like a lightning bolt, stretching toward the surface, right to where my hands had been. The jagged line made the whole thing look like an egg that was dropped.

As we watched, the crack repaired itself, the barrier stitching itself back together until it looked like nothing had happened and the tiny glimmer of brown dirt and blue sky vanished from sight.

"Great, so still trapped."

"For now," Ilyan said, his accent thick as he helped me back to my feet. "Something that can be cracked can also be broken."

"True."

My mind was buzzing with the possibility, of course most of those involved using something else besides my still aching hands as a conduit. I had a feeling those joints were going to bruise.

"You guys okay down there?" Risha called from above, her round face peering over the edge of the crater I had created to stare at us.

Round face, blue shirt. Breaking the barrier wasn't the only vision I had about this day.

"Crap," I hissed as I pushed myself out of Ilyan's arms, ignoring the ache in my body as I pulled my magic to me and soared out of the crater, the thing much deeper than I had expected.

I didn't answer her. I didn't even look at her. I went into action, magic sparking at my fingers as I turned toward the alleys and streets that surrounded the courtyard, waiting for hundreds of Edmund's men to make their arrival.

Wyn and Ryland emerged from the igloo as Ilyan flung himself out of the hole to land right next to me, his magic pulsing through air and soul like a tether. Stubborn as I was, I was ignoring it.

"They are coming," I continued to spin in place, letting my magic swim through the air as I tried to find them, find the army that had to be heading our way. But there was nothing. Literally nothing around us. I didn't feel anything, I could barely see anything besides red bathed buildings and blood soaked streets, even the darkened alleys were a little more red than usual.

First, I can't see through the barrier and now touching the darn thing was giving me a temporary magic blackout. I shook my head like a dog, foolishly thinking that perhaps that would help but thanks to my aching joints nothing happened.

"What's coming?" Wyn asked in alarm, her voice far away as Ilyan pulled me away from my frantic searching, arm around my waist as he held me against him. It was a good thing seeing as everything was beginning to swim.

"Edmund's men, I saw them." The spinning was somehow getting worse, and Ilyan's arms didn't seem quite strong enough to stop it. Besides, he was spinning, too.

"They are on their way..." It was little more than a gasp.

"Do you see them?" Ilyan asked, his voice low and swallowed by Rylands instant panic.

"His men? How many? Do we have time to leave?"

"Yes... no..." I didn't even feel them. I wasn't seeing anything but black, and that spinning was getting worse. Can it just settle down enough that I can figure out what's going on?

"Is the shield intact?" Wyn asked, and my swimming panic turned to dread.

When the barrier had attacked me it had done more than fried my internal circuit breakers, it had broken the shield I had put around us. Cracked it like Edmunds barrier.

Except this one didn't crack. It freaking shattered.

We heard the scream before we saw them, the screech of the Vilỳ loud enough that it was emanating from a swarm large enough to take us all down.

"They are here," Ryland said, his eyes to the red sky, the black cloud that was making its way to us, our sights and sounds clearly visible thanks to the broken barrier. "We need to get out of here."

Vilỳ were not what was coming, there was something worse. But before I could say anything, Ryland and Risha had taken off into the sky, their bodies vanishing as they shielded themselves and headed back to the Castle.

Wait. What? This not how this was supposed to happen.

"What are you waiting for?" Wyn asked in a whisper, her body crouched in preparation to take off. "Let's get out of here before they reach us and something happens."

Ilyan and I could only look at each other, the same dread painting our eyes.

This was not what was supposed to happen.

"Don't let him get into your head," Ilyan whispered, running the tips of his fingers over the side of my face and stretching toward the mark, although the softness of his touch did not make contact.

The Vilỳs were enough. We didn't need to draw anyone closer with an eruption of magical lightning storm of love.

'We aren't calling it that,' Ilyan chuckled as he took off into the air, his hand tight around mine as he pulled me after him.

I let him drag me, his magic supporting me as I stared at the ruins of our attempt, at the crater that was slowly filling with mud so red that it looked like blood, at the bodies of the Vilỳ that were littered around it.

Almost exactly as I had seen in sight. Except Vilỳ instead of people, and none of us were to be seen.

Close, but not exact.

"Something happened." My heart ached, it pulled and tugged in confusion as Ilyan and I soared behind a building. His wide turn giving me one last view of the tiny courtyard and the dark figures that were tumbling into the crater in search of noise, or bodies. Or both.

More Vilỳ, probably. I swear those things were drawn to blood, or in this case mud.

That close to the barrier it was the same, both in color and in the lives of those that died tried to claw their way out.

It was an end that was looking more and more like a reality for us.

'How could I have been so wrong?'

'We will figure it out, my love.' I couldn't even summon the smile to agree with him.

7

SAIN

OVAILIA SASHAYED AWAY from me like the dancer she had trained to be so long ago. The high heels on those darn boots tapped loudly, the eyes of the few Vilẏ who had arrived to scope out our conversation watching as she left, waiting for the danger to leave so they could attack.

It only took one flying down, one spark of light and a loss of wings and the rest of them left me alone. Perhaps they could smell Edmund's magic on me, but it was never more than a few that attacked, which was a shame, because I enjoyed ripping the wings from their bodies.

The smell of the Vilẏs acidic blood drenched the air, mixing with the smell of rot as Ovailia vanished, stuttering to the opposite end of the city, or barrier. I still wasn't sure how they managed to get in and out when neither mine nor Ilyan's magic had figured it out, but I was sure I could convince Ovailia to let me in on that secret without too much effort.

It was another piece to the puzzle that I needed to secure.

"Beautiful Ovailia." I soothed, watching the spot where

she had vanished long after she had gone. I watched it until my head throbbed and a low burn of sight heated at the base of my neck.

Something was about to happen.

I closed my eyes briefly and peeked into the sight, watching the images that Joclyn had seen earlier in the day unfold. The five of them, near the barrier. They had begun their silly "pop the barrier" plan earlier than expected, possibly to deter me from crashing their party. Made sense to the overly trusting king and queen. I was safely tucked away in my room after all.

Just like that, all the fantasy and lust that my visit with Ovailia had got me drunk on vanished like a bad hangover, leaving me with a hostile anger that was pounding against head and soul in an attempt to explode.

Ilyan and his Queen.

For centuries I had played into the hands and plans of others. I had given into their desires in the attempt of a greater goal. But that had gone too far, too long, and now they felt as if they could send me to my room like some toddler in a temper tantrum. Those of the first had never been treated in such a way, the first were not meant to be treated in such a way.

Ilyan's kingdom understood that, the Skříteks and Chosen that followed him saw me for what I was. I would make him see that too, I would show him what it means to rule a people.

"Bastard King isn't fit to command a snail. His parents never honored the world they were bred in. He doesn't know the meaning of loyalty. I will just have to teach him." The promise ripped through the air and brought another foolish Vilỳ to my side, the tattered brown creature crumpling into the alley with a spark of my magic flung right into the gnarled twisted leather of his forehead.

The look of shock on the tiny thing's face was a perfect replica of the look Ilyan would give me when all of this was over. Now that was a future I couldn't wait to create.

But I would have to start with my darling daughter and her unreliable sights.

'Make her doubt herself.'

"As you wish Ovailia." I followed her path, knowing there was no way to catch up with her. She wasn't my target. Ilyan and his posse and their plans to destroy Edmund's barrier were not that far ahead.

They may have tried to ban me, but they couldn't keep me away, they had begun their plan early, and I knew why.

Earlier today, the image of them near the barrier had sweltered my sight, only to repeat itself when I projected the future of that poor boy. The five of them near the barrier, watching as Edmund's men swam through the barrier like mice from a hole. Seeing the men enter would be just what they needed to find a way out, and I wasn't ready for that to happen. Not yet.

I needed that information before they did.

Destroying their chance to infiltrate the barrier would not only keep them locked under my influence for a bit longer, but do exactly what needed to be done and force Joclyn to question her sight. Poor girl trusts what she sees so much, I couldn't resist another opportunity to make her question it.

Perhaps then she could go to her room and think about what she had done.

I was instantly fuming again, the anger pushing me forward as I dodged behind one building and then another in my trek to the edge of the barrier. My sight grew as warm as the air as I approached the edge of the dome and the greenhouse it had created.

Everything was hot both inside and out as I smothered myself with a shield, blocking my body from view as I approached the courtyard, and the mysteriously floating rocks and rubble that were stacking themselves near the edge of the courtyard.

The fools.

They had shrouded themselves and much of the noise, although mumbles were seeping through the shield and bouncing off the tall buildings around them, they might as well not have shielded themselves at all. It was easy enough to see who had created this mistaken attempt at protection. If she couldn't even create a shield, what business did she have dabbling in the art of the Drak?

She would never be worthy enough for me to teach her, even if I had wanted to.

I would never allow it.

I watched the ridiculous floating rocks a moment longer before I stepped behind one of the tall white buildings beside them, toward the other and nearly identical courtyard that the attack was due to begin in. The buildings were the same, the benches and dying trees in the exact same position. Under the deep red light of the barrier it was near impossible to tell the difference. But any Drak should have been able to feel the difference. She should have been able to see it.

"Ridiculous half-breed." Making her doubt herself was going to be easier than I think even Ovailia assumed.

The ground beneath my feet heated and I lifted myself a foot off the ground. Wynifred must be melting that barrier of hers. It was the only part of their plan that made sense.

Until I saw the ember glow of the stones beneath me.

Thousands of years and none of them knew how to be discreet.

The ancient cobbled street cooled as dark shapes formed on the other side of the barrier. It didn't matter how close you got, you could barely make out what was happening in the world on the other side, and this was no exception.

Dark masses weaved through the wall, the shapes moving closer as the magic in the air sizzled, Joclyn's vile heat mixing with something that I wasn't sure even she could differentiate.

The shimmer in the air multiplied as the wall waved and moved. Like someone had thrown a stone into a pond on the other side of the courtyard.

Joclyn.

The waves rocked like the ocean in a storm as the dark shapes shifted, as though they were causing the ripple and not the foolish attempt at magic in the courtyard next door. The shapes began to take shape as the waves pulled into a tide pool, although the deepening ridges were no longer coming from the other side of the buildings.

The ripples of water shifted until the circle of impact moved to the stretch of red barrier right in front of me, and the shapes just behind them.

Straightening my spine, my magic snapped away from me like a rubber band, smothering not just me but the entire alley in a shield that would keep Joclyn and the others from seeing what was about to happen. I would have to take them down as quickly and quietly as I could.

The dark masses grew arms and legs as a blast shook the ground, the barrier, and the building to my left. The ripples in the barrier ripped apart under whatever had caused the blast, the tears spreading into a gaping hole, like a porthole in a cruise ship.

More than twenty of Edmund's deranged chosen flooded through the barrier without looking, their faces filtered with panic as they entered the city that they had been told spelled danger.

They tumbled over each other, trying to find their footing before they turned, back to the wall and the now closed opening with horror on their faces. Everything from wide eyes, chattering teeth, and worse plagued them. I was sure that one was crying.

Perfect.

"Hello." Keeping my voice calm, I pulled their focus away from the barrier as the shocked shout of Ilyan and Wyn lifted through the buildings. So much for whatever Joclyn had done to mask their sound, her barrier had clearly broken. This was about to get a whole lot more interesting.

Edmund's shell-shocked minions turned toward the sound, their confusion mounting as they looked between me and the voices. I guess Edmund, or whoever had sent them through the barrier, hadn't truly prepared them for what would be waiting. They seemed about as lost as the other of the firsts when we had emerged from the Mud. Screaming. Howling. Dumb.

I was always amazed they had been able to rule as well as they did.

"Are you supposed to kill them?" I nodded towards the voices as another shout drifted over to us. That one sounded like Ryland. "Or are you supposed to kill me?"

The depth of my voice roamed free for the first time in centuries. Well, besides as it had with Dramin for the last month, but I would never hide anything from my son. The chosen however, looked even more confused as the voices of the others picked up again.

Their eyes darted between me, the disembodied voices, and the tallest of the Chosen; a blonde man who stood right in front. He seemed to have taken on the role of leader.

"What do you choose?" I asked, right to the blonde.

"That depends on who you are," The man said, cracking his knuckles and letting some of his diseased and broken magic fall to the ground. "Are you with our King Edmund or are you with the bastard Ilyan."

"I am with neither." They weren't expecting that answer, the powerful glare of their ringleader faded, his magic slowing to a single spark of green that dripped down to the cobbles like sludge.

"Excuse me?" He asked, turning to those around him as if they would have the answer, but they looked as confused as he did.

"I serve no master but myself and accept no master other than me. If you do not stand with me, then you will stand below this earth and be returned to the wells of Imdalind from which I was born."

It felt good to give that threat. It felt good to let my voice raise and tremble through both the ground and the spines of the fools that stood before me. I could even see their legs shake as I stepped closer, as the angry screech of Vilÿs followed behind. The creatures were coming, and this was about to get a whole lot more interesting.

Even the miniature army that Edmund had sent through the barrier for slaughter knew the scream of the flying bats, and they were just as scared of them as Ilyan and his followers were.

"Which master will you serve?" I asked in a hiss, taking another slow calculated step toward the group, listening to

Ilyan's heightened command. The blonde turned toward the sound before turning back to me, the confusion was so deep in him now that he may not have understood the world at all.

"Will you cross beyond this building and destroy Ilyan and his men? They are right there." They all stepped toward the still heightening voices, their confusion replaced by eagerness.

Each and every one of them was ready to rush the man and end him in the name of their master. It truly was a shame that they all believed they had a chance, that none of them realized they were little more than sheep sent to the slaughter by a cruel king.

I would never do that as long as the right allegiances were served. If they weren't? I had a feeling that all of these poor souls were about to discover the dark side of my loyalty.

"Or will you stay with me and forsake them both for the true ruler of this world?" I had expected the confusion on the blonde man's face to deepen, to furrow his brow and ask why he should stand with me.

Instead, the confusion was only anger, his scowl deepening as he stepped away from the group and closer to me.

"Ilyan isn't over there, is he?" He snarled, narrowing his eyes as he let the magic drip again. The pathetic attempt at an attack wasn't even worth a cringe. "They warned us you would say things like that. They warned us you would try to lure us away with only the intent on ending us. We won't fall for it!"

His voice was too loud, and I could only hope that Ilyan and his sheep were loud enough in whatever argument they were currently thrown in to hear the shout and the answering grunts and groans from his companions as they stepped up to join him, their own magic dripping pathetically from their fingers.

"Surrender, Ilyan! We are taking you to our master whether you like it or not. You can come with us without recourse or you can come in pieces, the choice is up to you!" He roared the recited warning as he lifted his fist, looking at me with fire in his eyes. The look was full of too much fear for me to take it seriously.

All of the men and the few women behind him did the same, their determination was clear. They didn't stand a chance against me; their chances would have actually been better if I was Ilyan. He was enough of a blubbering fool that he would try to barter and convince them to come over to 'his side'.

I didn't have time for such foolishness. I, instead, laughed with a mockery that cut through their false confidences like a blunted knife, stabbing them hard as a few of them stumbled back, looking towards the barrier as if it would magically open again for them.

"Odd. I wasn't aware I had long blonde hair and haughty accent that makes teen girls swoon. No matter. If you will not stand with me, then I doubt anyone will have any use for you."

Their magic dripped to the ground, splashing against the cobbles like rot. Mine, however, sparked with a snap of my fingers, a brilliant green flame lifting from my palm in a swirl of lightning that twisted over my skin, reflecting off their shocked faces as the flow of their power dropped.

"I'm sorry to have to do this," I said as the orb swelled to the size of a small child and I dropped it against the ground. It hit against stone and asphalt with the rattle of a bomb, the lightning inside of it swelling until it swallowed us all and we stood not in the red tinted world of Edmund's barrier, but the lightning green of mine.

The ill-trained Chosen screamed and cowered, their magic forgotten as shock hit them and any sign of training was swallowed by their very mortal fear. Their panic grew as the orb did until it pressed against my pre-cast shield, the powerful barrier concealing us from Joclyn and the mission they were still attempting to complete. One courtyard over, and they couldn't see us. They could no longer hear us.

No one who cared could hear their screams.

"I am sure you all have quite a bit of potential. But I simply can't have my daughter grasp her ability any more than she has," I continued over the sounds of their fear, flexing my hand before me as I tested the control of the attack, tested my magic. It had been years since I had used this particular spell, it felt good to stretch the strength of it again.

"I am sure you understand." Their screams were dying down now, the blonde's magic beginning to spark again as he stepped away from the others, his panic making his magic uncontrollable. Uncontrollable, but not undefeatable.

"Your daughter? Joclyn?" He asked, pulling my focus away from my hand, and the flexing fingers that were moving in time with the pulsing constriction of the dome, not that any of the Chosen were paying enough attention to notice. "You are Sain. We are Edmund's men! We are on your side!"

His proclamation silenced the others, their screams fading to pants and tired pleas as they closed in, the look in their eyes clear they expected their salvation. Did anyone in the world have more than a little sense?

"Then you weren't listening. I serve no master but myself and accept no master other than me. You had your chance."

There was only a glimpse of their fear, of their shock, before I closed my hand into a fist, and constricted the green globe around them. The magic passed through me with a gust of wind and a sway of power. The others were not so lucky. With a faint pop and the clatter of bones, their charred skeletons fell to the ground. There was nothing left of the overconfident Chosen but a few hundred charred bones and the shadow of their screams as my magic absorbed them.

As I brought their magic into me, back to where it belonged.

Disappointing. I will have to try something with more fight next time. With a sigh, I turned to leave, ready to take off into the sky and beat Ilyan home. They were already ahead of me though, I could see his blonde mop of hair and the long lines of gold as he burst into the sky. His hand was wrapped around Joclyn's and the two of them were unshielded for a moment before both building and magic pulled them from my view.

I would have to hurry to beat them back. It shouldn't be a problem, however. I could jump through air with the look that was now burned into me. Joclyn, staring back at the courtyard. Confused. Hurt. Broken.

Her sight had not come true. Her sight was nothing more than a pile of bones behind me. A pile of bones and broken sights. If she could defy the sacred visions for her benefit, then I would do the same for mine. I had done it before, and would do it again.

"Go to your room, little girl. It's time to think about what you have done, and just how wrong you are. Just how powerless you are against me."

8

OVAILIA

IT HAD BEEN a productive morning for the rescue teams, it seems. A hundred new arrivals were lined up like cattle, rope tied between them as they cowered beside the chain link fence that at one point had separated this farm from another. Now it was a line to determine who had lived long enough to be welcomed into Edmund's presence. Who would be of use to him?

Men, women, and a few children stood and shivered in the chilly autumn breeze, their naked bodies on display to the two Trpaslíks that Edmund had granted the role as trainer. It was a position that hadn't been needed for centuries, and these two had been part of the many who were more than eager to take up the mantle.

They were clearly enjoying themselves with the number of screams that were drifting from the line.

Every few minutes someone else would shout out as a magical attack hit them, the power strong enough to gauge the strength and ability of the magic that the poisoned Vilỳ had awakened. They either rose quickly, a sure sign their magic was strong and ready, or they cowered and cried and were disposed of within minutes.

It only took a few deaths before those with constitutions strong enough to be of use to us began to stand out from the others.

Another scream, this one a male, followed by the shriek of a little girl as the man fell to the ground. The man was her father with how she was yanking against the rope, begging him to stand. The foolish child didn't even see the other attack before it had hit her in the back, sending her down to the ground alongside the old man.

He didn't get up, I was surprised to see that she did. A bit more angry and revenge filled than we would like to see, but the trainers let it pass. That was a call I would have to let them make. If she wasn't up to the task, she would find herself under the dirt.

Passing this test didn't bring out the banners of welcome to Edmund's army. Especially for a child her age. She would be lucky if she passed the training that came after this. Any of them would be lucky to pass the next step. Or even the one after that.

"Basking in the sound of the dead and dying?" I asked as I approached the broad shoulders of my father, the man barely taking notice of my arrival, or the line of people thirty yards behind him. His eyes were forward, on the twenty chosen that had made it past the fence, only to be beaten into submission and branded as his property.

The burn went past flesh and into the bone, no wonder there was so much screaming over here.

"Did you give him his task?" He asked, his brow furrowing as another one of the chosen fell to the ground, the way he was twitching made it clear that he wasn't going to get up any time soon.

"I did, he seemed amicable. I expect we will have the information we need soon. His tongue is still tied in relation to my darling brother, but I placed a tracker on him. We should know soon."

Edmund's smile spread briefly, before he turned from the branding and toward the massive pit he was building as the main arena for training. He took off at a near sprint, both I, and his brand new set of trained Chosen bodyguards struggling to keep up.

The structure was quickly turning into his pride and joy. He wanted to watch his army unfold, and he was creating the largest and gaudiest thing to do it. Although, seeing as it was only steel pipe and scaffolding right now, I had no idea what it would look like when done.

The whole thing could have been done by now, but he was using the old Egyptian method to train his fighters. Slaves first, glorified Chosen later.

"I hope by soon you mean in hours," Edmund growled in warning, ducking underneath the slat of heavy burlap that was serving as a door.

He didn't even hold the thing open for me. I was clearly on his bad side.

"I expect the answer anytime, unless the spell or shield that is blocking Ilyan's camp from view burns my tether." You would think that Ilyan wouldn't be foolish enough to let such a simple spell sneak past his defenses, but I knew my brother. The man was prideful enough to let things slip past his better judgement. Like Sain, and me, and the filthy little gold digger.

"And if it does?" He asked as we entered what looked like a round amphitheater, metal bleachers surrounding a massive pit. "What will you do then?"

"Then the Vilỳ I tasked to follow him will lead me right

back." Assuming Sain doesn't kill them, it had been foolish of me to teach him the failsafe for the little buggers. But I needed him alive, and he was too weak to even look the nasty little things in the eye.

Edmund turned to me, his displeasure clear and I straightened, pulling my shoulders into a taught little line in expectation of his rage.

It never came. It was drowned by the scream of one of the Chosen in the pit that had been carved into the middle of his monstrosity, the rage instantly redirected on whatever was below.

A string of profanity ripped from him, the vulgarities followed by a ribbon of magic the color of pitch. His guards tensed in fear, the man closest to me visibly shaking in expectation of Edmund's magic destroying him for nothing more than shuffling his feet. Which he had done, he had reason to be concerned, but he should know better than to react.

I didn't even move, I stood still, watching the magic plunge itself into one of the trainers in the pit below, the man having killed a man out of frustration and not out of training as he had been instructed.

"Fool!" Edmund roared, one of his curls coming loose from his neatly streaked back style as he jumped over the bleachers that were still being constructed and into the sand pits below.

The bleachers shook from the weight, the place more of a construction zone than I expected. I am sure it had something to do with the dwindling number of Chosen. The more they killed, the less of his disposable army he had to do his bidding. It was going much slower than I think anyone expected.

Especially him. My father was not a patient man.

"What are you waiting for? Go after him!" The guards jerked at my command, the three men jostling around before they bolted over the edge of the bleachers like a herd of elephants who had high aspirations to be monkeys.

Fools.

I don't know what my father was thinking assigning these bumbling idiots to be his guard. Just like the Chosen, he had gone through a few too many of them in his rage of impatience. I wasn't sure if the last set had survived his outbursts, I knew of one that was still in the hospital.

Straightening my leather jacket and trying to ignore the scuff that covered the toe of my brand new thigh-high boots, I bolted after them landing lithely in the sand with nothing more than a swing of my hair, which I expertly flipped so as to replace the few strands that had fallen out of line.

"I will end all of you if this behavior keeps up!" Edmund was in full roar, his hair having completely come loose as he screamed, red faced, at the remaining Trpaslík trainers, the few Chosen that had survived up to this point were absolutely trembling in fear as the blood of both the Chosen and now the Trpaslík seeped into the sand, staining it red.

The scuff and mud that had been on the toe of my boots before was swallowed by sand as I stepped toward my father, the loose sand attempting to swallow me to my ankles. It only took a bit of magic to keep me from sinking to oblivion. Something the poor little battered chosen couldn't even muster. Tons of magic inside of them and they couldn't even perform a simple elevation.

Edmund was right to be angry. I wasn't sure what anyone had been doing to train the Chosen over the last few weeks.

"We are doing as you asked, my king." One of the trainers was foolish enough to respond, and even though his voice was trembling as much as his hands, no amount of prostrate apologies was going to keep him alive. He would have been better off to keep his trap shut.

"Really? You are doing as I have asked?" Edmund's voice seeped with a darkness so intense that I could have sworn the iciness in the air was from him and not from the impending winter.

Luckily, this time the man was smart enough not to retort against the king, but the damage was done.

"I did not ask you to kill my army before I had a chance to use them!" Edmund roared, the wind picking up as his magic did, the chill growing even deeper as the black tar of his power flooded from the palm of his hand and flew toward the Chosen that was openly weeping.

The other trainer fell to the ground, his hands over his head as if it would protect him, the Chosen screeched and tried to back away, to escape whatever was about to happen, but whatever binding had been placed around them kept them still, forcing them to watch as the head of the man who had spoken to the King was ripped clean off in a shower of red rain.

"Damn it," I grumbled, wiping my hand against jacket and shirt in a hope to chase away the bright drops of red that were trying to seep their way into the fabric. I was too late.

So much for keeping these jeans looking nice.

"I am so tired of these pathetic Trpaslíks believing that they..." Edmund's voice was loud, but the Chosen off to the side was even louder.

His terrorized scream ripped through the air, echoing off the walls of the arena and bouncing around with a sound that I had only heard a few times before. Mostly right before I killed someone. I had enough tension wound through my spine after meeting with Sain that this one could easily follow that trend.

It would be easy.

Hell, it would be fun.

I stepped toward him slowly, narrowing my eyes as my magic sparked at the tips of my fingers. He was so focused on Edmund that he didn't see each slow, calculated step I made toward him. And when he did, it was too late.

His screams picked up as he turned to me, hands and legs working fast in his attempt to scuttle away through the sand like a crab. The bindings still held tightly, however, and he barely moved more than a few inches. Forced to watch my magic spark, and my lips curl into a smile as I began to laugh.

"What did I tell you about playing with your food, Ovailia," Edmund whispered, his voice soft in my ear.

"Chew slow or fast, just make sure you chew."

Heat and air sent a shiver over my neck, my smile stretching as his large hand wrapped around my shoulder and pulled me to a stop. The heat of his magic seeped through the heavy leather of my jacket until I could smell the fabric, the acidic tar of burning flesh almost as homely as the poor guys screams, the sounds having picked up when Edmund joined my advance.

"I think these ones haven't been trained properly. Best to start over from scratch." His frustration was clear, but even I couldn't disagree. This one was screaming like a child with only one tiny spray of blood against his cheek. What good was he to be for us?

"Dispose of them both?" If I wasn't going to play with them long, I was going to make this little bit the best I could. A few sparks of scarlet magic to match the drips of red that were slowly drying against their cheeks.

The screamer continued to fight his way away from us, in vain. Although the other one was staring at the magic, his jaw dropping as if he had never seen the likes before. What had they been doing with them if he hadn't seen a few sparks?

I don't know how either of them made it past the fence.

"Make it hurt." Edmund's whisper rustled over my skin, prompting me forward and my magic into overdrive as I postured the writhing, pathetic, useless men.

"If you think you are screaming now..."

"Wait!" The other one called out as he tried to stand, only to be pushed back down by the magical binding and land face-first in the sand. "Wait." He repeated, pushing himself back up less than a second later, speaking through a mouth of sand and blood.

"Wait. Don't kill me!" He was on his knees now, clasping his hands before him like he was praying to Edmund and I. Well, begging for his life anyway. It was a look that more of the little dung beetles should adopt.

"We have a beggar! How fun!" I shrieked, letting my magic drip into the sand and sparking tiny little fires around my boots. I didn't even look, and the begging slave before me didn't flinch, but the eyes of the now silent screamer were so wide I could see the fire reflected in their depth.

"I like playing with those the most." The prodding glee wasn't even masked as a threat, the warning was clear, but the man didn't flinch or cower. He stayed still, on his knees, his hands clasped before him.

Heart thundering in eager need to watch this guy's head spin, I took another step closer, letting the magic drip again. Still, he did not flinch, he continued his plea, not a single tear leaking from his ugly brown eyes.

"Please my...my lady. Edmund. The King... my king... he

said he didn't want to waste any more of us. Of my kind. Let me show you what I can do." For a man begging for his life, his voice a was firmer than I would expect.

Determined, maybe. Everything about him was... interesting.

"And what are you suggesting?" Edmund stepped right beside me, his hand wrapping around my wrist and stopping the flow of my magic. This time I didn't mind, I wanted to see how this one panned out.

Crossing my arms, I took a tiny step back, letting my boots seep into the sand, content to watch whatever show was about to play out. The foolishness of a mortal man when they believe they have nothing to lose.

"It's clear you want fighters. And we can give you fighters," the begging man began, the screamer looking between his comrade and his king with blood shot eyes, the tiniest bit of hope springing from the black of iris's. He was a fool if he thought his friends arguments were going to favor him. He had sealed his fate with his scream. "They may not have trained us, but your power, your gift, is still inside of us. Let us show you what we can do. Please. A life for a life."

"You are quite the little flatterer, aren't you?" Edmund spoke to the man as one would an encourageable toddler, bending over to get a better look at him. It was clear he had been through a bit, and had the bruises and few cuts. He had no blood on him now, however. Not yet.

"What are you suggesting?"

"Let us fight. Whoever kills the other gets to live. Whoever kills the other gets to continue training for your army."

Edmund slowly pulled himself to standing, shock bathing his features as he looked down at the beggar. Meanwhile the other man had begun to yell again, his pleas for mercy, for safety sounding like the high pierced shriek of a rabbit before slaughter.

I had worked under my father for a long time. I had done his bidding, killed thousands. I had never heard a bargain quite as brazen as this. Even I was focused on Edmund, waiting to see what he would decide.

"Granted."

One word, and a snap of his fingers and I felt the magic in the arena fall away. The screaming man turned, attempting to find his feet and run away. The other was on him before he could move more than a foot, his untrained magic dripping from his fingertips like tar.

"No!" The screaming man yelled as the others magic hit him, his escape foiled as he twisted in the sand in an attempt to fight back, in one final and pitiful endeavor to save himself.

It didn't matter. The hands of the fighter wrapped around the screamer and his shrieks filled the area again. This time, they lasted only minutes before another fan of blood sprayed over us, and the scream was silenced with the crack of bone and the ripping of flesh.

Silence screamed through the air as the winner rose, holding the head of the screaming man by the hair as he stepped forward, extending the head out to Edmund before falling to one knee, severed head out, his head bowed.

There was only the drip of blood against sand, only the muffled reverences of the winner. Then there was the boisterous laugh of my father, the massive man throwing the severed head into the sand as he lifted the victor to his feet, the man's face terrified as he looked from my father to me.

He was as much of a fool as his companion if he thought

I was going to step in and save him. I would sooner see him dead. My father had other plans.

"Ovailia," he boomed. "Stop the training. Take all those poor souls at the fence and throw them in the tent. I believe I have found a much more entertaining and effective way to train. We are going to do it as it once was, as the Trpaslíks have done for centuries.

I want to watch these fools fight to the death."

9
___

JOCLYN

I WASN'T ABOUT to call myself a failure, but I wasn't happy with myself either. Or rather, I wasn't happy with the wonky sight issues that I couldn't escape. That much was clear as I charged down the hallway like a baby rhinoceros, Ilyan hot on my heels. The two of us looked like those angry royals that I had seen on cable TV at Ry's house once upon a time.

We were both still covered in dirt, and seeing as we had been soaked with water not too long ago, I wasn't sure we could pass for any kind of royals right then, angry or not.

The amount of confused stares that we were getting made it clear we looked less like powerful royals and more like angry trolls who emerged out of a cave collapse.

Ilyan may not be as endlessly frustrated as I was, but he was more worried than he was trying to pass off. So, we charged right to the only person I really trusted, and the only person who could truly help.

'It isn't that bad, mi lasko.'

'You do realize you have rubble on your shoulder, right?' I gave him a side glance as we turned the corner and sure

enough, he was wiping off the tiny bits of rock that had been trying to build a bird's nest there.

This hallway was emptier than the last. Although I half expected to run into Wyn. She was with Thom every spare moment she could get, after all. Thankfully, I could feel from here that the room was empty.

I don't know what it was about the barrier and my magic, but after we had flown a few blocks away all my tracking and sight and everything had come buzzing back. I could feel the majority of the magic of the city in detail, including the fact that Dramin's room was empty.

Having Wyn there would have been fine, but there was one other person I didn't want to come in contact with on this excursion. Unfortunately for us, he turned the corner ahead when we were only steps from the door.

"Sain!" Ilyan boomed, he was far more pleasant than I could bustle up right then. I was barely able to conceal my scowl. Which was fine, because my father was in a full on scowl too, giving me one dead eyed stare before he pulled his face back into a smile, looking between Ilyan and I as if his anger had never existed.

"My lord, My lady." He sounded nice enough, and he even bowed, which gave me a great deal of confidence for what was about to happen.

'Is that sarcasm I hear?' Ilyan teased, I stubbornly ignored him and took one big step forward, facing my father head on.

"Sain." Right then I was super glad that the old man didn't have a title of his own. It was kind of awesome being able to refer to him as 'guy number one' and not the first of his kind or whatever.

I may love it, but he hated it. His eyes twitched a bit, his nostrils flaring as he tried to keep his smile on his face.

"What brings you here?" Ilyan asked as he stepped beside me, the calm touch of his fingers against my elbow sending one shot of soothing magic into me. If only it was enough to calm my temper. It would be so worth it to fight him right now.

"My son," Sain nodded to the door that stood like some sort of prize between us, his smile making a grand return. "He is expecting me. I have told him I would give him an update as to what happened this morning and to how the Chosen reacted to the magic of our kind."

I hoped I was hallucinating the snap that he put on the word 'our'. It was good he wasn't looking at me, because my scowl had deepened so much that I would probably never be able to banish it. My fingers flexed against the dirt covered denim of my jeans, clinging to anything I could so as not to swing punches, or magic, or whatever I wanted to do in a fight.

"Of course, it looks like you two have been in quite a bit of trouble since then." Sain's lip curled as he looked us up and down, as though he was proud of himself for something.

"How did the operation at the barrier go? You are both here, so I expect it wasn't quite the smashing success you had been hoping. Was Joclyn's sight able to help?"

'You know, it wouldn't be a shame if that wall collapsed onto him...'

'I think the people who live in this hall and prefer the use of doors would find it to be a shame.' My stony exterior cracked at that, a tiny smile peeking out and catching Sain's focus. He looked between us, understanding what was going on and expecting some kind of explanation, not like he was going to get one.

Ilyan and I stood side by side, staring him down like he was the scum on the bottom of our shoe.

'I prefer the image of a bug on a windshield. Smeared by the wipers.' That time he got a laugh, the tiny snicker acting like an ignition switch and any attempt at looking agreeable faded, Sain turning into the grumpy old man that I knew so well.

"If you will excuse me." He took a step forward, expecting to barge into Thom and Dramin's room and lock the door behind him. Unfortunately, he was barely able to take a single step before Ilyan was in his way, his tall lanky figure towering over the Drak.

"We will gladly excuse you," Ilyan boomed, loud enough that the few people who had begun to filter in the hall scattered like frightened mice. "We have business here. I assume you can make yourself useful elsewhere."

"Ilyan you can't be serious," Sain said with the slightest of stutter, backpedaling into the subservient mongrel so fast he might have been slapped there. "You can't keep me from my son."

"He can when it concerns the Queen requesting an audience with her brother." I announced using the most regal voice that I owned. "With her brother alone."

I tacked on that last bit when he opened his mouth to fight me, and instead left him gasping like a fish. His eyes were hard little specks of green as he looked between us, searching for cracks.

We had both been through enough today that he really didn't want to do that.

"As you wish, My Lord. I will return at a later time." There wasn't a drop of true courtesy in his voice, it was as cold as stone, just like the look in his eyes.

He smacked his heels together before bolting down the

hall with what I could have sworn was a hiss and swear. With all his 'my lords' and 'my ladies', there wasn't even a tiny head bow like so many of the others gave us. There was, however, a glare that I was sure was meant to melt my face off, hidden as he rounded the corner.

I was starting to think I wasn't as childish as I thought.

"He keeps getting better and better," I mumbled as I covered the hall and the room in a shield that would zap anyone, specifically Sain, if they were dumb enough to try to cross.

"At least we won't have to deal with his face melting glares." I would gladly wipe that away and exchange it for the swoon-worthy wink Ilyan was giving me.

I turned with a smile, opening the door to Dramin's room with the faintest of knocks.

I knew he wouldn't be asleep, or in any other position than he normally was. He lay on his bed, as usual, propped up by a mound of pillows, his eyes hooded as he read a book I had brought him last week. Although, with the way his eyes were glossed over I wasn't sure if he was reading it at all.

"Hi Uncle," I said, pulling his attention as Ilyan slipped in behind me and shut and locked the door, using his own brand of magic to keep undesirables out.

Ilyan gave Dramin a nod as the man looked up, before he took off to where Thom was still unconscious. He had his own brother to see, after all.

"Child," Dramin greeted me with a smile, the dull light in his eyes sparking back to life as he pat the bed beside him. "I feel as if I haven't seen you in ages."

"It's been a few days."

"Ages," he repeated, his voice a very clear reprimand. I wanted to tell him that my absence was more caused by his bodyguard than by my inability to get my butt over here, but I had a feeling he already knew.

"It feels like ages," I said with a sigh, "I will give you that."

Dramin must have heard the frustration in my voice because his face fell and he leaned back on the pillows with a sigh of his own, reaching for the empty earthen mug on his bedside table. Although he made no move to fill it with Black Water.

"You are carrying the world on your shoulders again, child." Dramin reached over his starched blankets for my hand, his open palm as inviting as Ilyan's open arms. I didn't hesitate to place my hand in his.

"It's more like the world barreled me over and I don't know which way is up anymore." Dramin narrowed his focus, not understanding what I was trying to say.

"Tell me what happened."

With anyone else but Dramin and Ilyan I might have to steel my confidence, straighten my shoulders, and get on with it. The genuine calm that flowed off Dramin had no need for that, however.

"It's my sight. And Sain."

"Father." I didn't like the way he corrected me, but I nodded none-the-less. Dramin may have a better relationship with our father, but he still stood up to him for me.

"What has happened with your sight, child?" He asked, squeezing my hand and sandwiching it between his own with the tiniest of pressure.

"I saw something, three different ways. And all of them happened," I hesitated. That wasn't right. I pushed out a cleansing sigh and glanced at Ilyan, knowing he was listening even if his focus was only on his brother.

"Parts of them happened. Parts of each one. I don't agree with Sain, but something is wrong."

Dramin's grey-green eyes held nothing but kindness, his bull-dog face holding the tiniest bit of a smile, but it wasn't in mocking. It was in understanding, that alone was enough to lift the weight off my shoulders.

I hadn't even realized I had been carrying it around.

"Is that all, child? What else has happened?"

I sighed, sagged back against the bed until my back hit the footrest and asked what I had come here for in the beginning.

"It's not what happened, it's what I need your help to do."

"And what is that?"

"I need to learn the ways of the Drak." Sain's wording tasted like bile as I said it, but there was no going back now. The words were out, littering the air like vermin that even Dramin hated. His lips were pressed into a tight line, his usually happy and calm demeanor seemingly punctured by my question.

There went my usual calm, every muscle tightened so fast I was sure Ilyan could hear the snap, especially with how he jumped to attention, his hand still wrapped around Thom's as he questioned me. I waved him off, he needed to settle down. He couldn't always rush to my rescue.

"Where is this coming from?" Dramin asked with a bark that fit his face. There wasn't even a hint of laughter in those few words, my muscles tightened further.

This wasn't like him, but I couldn't back down now. Although I did check the room and everything around us to make sure that Sain was not here. Lucky us, everything seemed clear.

"From being a Drak and wanting to know more?" My

question sounded like it had a question inside of it, I wasn't sure how to answer that.

"No," Dramin's voice dropped own to a whisper, the bed creaking as he leaned toward me. "Tell me what really happened, child. At the fountain."

He knew. He knew about the fountain, and everything stunk because of it. I didn't want to admit that I had been set up, but I had very clearly been set up.

'Tell him.' Ilyan prompted.

Wyn was indifferent about Sain, Ryland would defend him if I ever said anything bad, and Dramin? There were times when I was sure that Dramin was scared of Sain.

This was sure chalking up to be one of those times.

"Sain was calling sight in a pillar of water, I had never seen anything like it before. He asked me to join and..." I let my explanation fade off, I wasn't interested in explaining more than that. Dramin was nodding so hard he seemed to understand.

"So that's what he was planning," he mumbled, causing Ilyan to jerk up and take a step toward us.

"What was he planning, Dramin?" Ilyan asked, but Dramin only smiled and waved him off.

"Never you mind, young king, we have bigger Drak matters to handle, now," His smiled drifted from Ilyan to me as he held my hand, giving it a gentle tug as he pulled me up to him. "What did you see child?"

"A whole lot of things that didn't end up happening. And a whole lot of things that did. The Vilỳ around a crater. A fight near the red wall. Risha in a very specific shirt." I gave another sigh. "If Sain keeps going on about how I am breaking things then I might end up having to believe him. I need to know more about what I am so that I can be what I am supposed to be."

I wasn't even sure if that made sense to me, but Dramin was nodding vigorously now, a smile on his face as he patted my hand.

"I would love to teach you. To help you know your sight as I once knew mine."

The smile had faded by the time he had finished his sentence, his hands tightening as he pulled me even closer to him.

"Then tell me what I am doing wrong, Uncle."

"You are doing nothing wrong, child," Dramin said with a pat of my hand, placing it back on the starched sheets as he leaned back, lifting the mug from where it was nestled in his lap. "I will show you. I assumed you have shielded the room?"

I gave him a nod.

"Perfect. Then call sight to you."

Dramin handed me the mug, his eyes eager, almost as if he was more hungry for my vision than he was for the water.

The mug felt like all the others, there was nothing special about that, but the way both Dramin and Ilyan were looking at me, with so much expectation in their eyes, the silly thing might have weighed near a ton in my hands.

"And how do I do that? I drink Black Water all day long." If there was such a thing as skeptical eyes, Dramin was currently on the receiving end of them.

"You must drink with the intention of obtaining sight."

Nothing about what he said made sense, but my magic was whispering inside of me, pulling me toward the mug. My power knew exactly what to do.

"So, I think about sight, drink, and--?"

"Sight will come." He chuckled that time and leaned back against the bed, his low laugh drowned out by the creak of the bed frame. "Do you remember the very first time we met, back in that drafty cave in the alps?" He tried to force another laugh, but it didn't come quite as easily that time.

"Yes. When you had me drink Black Water for the first time."

"And where I showed you the pool of sight. And you had sight for the first time." He tapped the ridge of the mug from where he lounged against the bed, sending it squeaking again. "It is the same concept here. The water is the same after all. It comes from the same well. From the same place of magic in the world. Bring it to you, bring it into you, and ask it to show you what you wish to see."

"For a second there I thought I was going to get some answers. I forgot that Drak speak in riddles." I prodded him with a smile, tracing the ridge of the mug as the old man answered with a chuckle. A thin layer of water trailed behind my touch, the black water slowly pooling in the bottom of the mug.

"You are one of us, child. Your mind understands these riddles. You know that water controls the power of your sight. Do not be afraid of it."

Is that what I was? Afraid of the water? Afraid of sight?

No.

That one I knew for sure. I had an idea of where the fear was coming from, however. Or rather the bristling anger.

Dramin was looking at me so intently that I didn't need to admit it out loud.

"This just got awkward."

I didn't have another choice, as irritating as it was. I had asked for this, I might as well see it through. I drank deep, trying to keep the sight in my mind, fully aware both Dramin and Ilyan were staring at me.

The longer this went on, the more I realized that the word awkward really didn't cover this. Bizarre almost seemed better.

This was bizarre.

My head began to spin, I wasn't sure what made this time different than every other time I had drank black water, but sight was already coming, and I wholeheartedly let it take me, following the ember burn of my sight into a vision that I had had earlier that day, when I had been sparring with Wyn.

Wyn ran down a street, horror and joy flashing over her face like a weird switch. Her expression kept switching, the flashes slowing until I realized that in joy she was covered in blood, and in fear she was covered in dirt. Two different moments.

"The turn is near, if you take the way that is before you." The words burst out in that same low monotone, but they didn't fill me with any of the excitement of sight. It was only fear as the image twisted into the cloaked runner, confusion as the words flowed, as the sight came faster.

As it changed.

There was so much about it that was different, the cloaked runner for example wasn't bolting down the same street as before. The cloak seemed more tattered than new.

"Beware the spark, for it alone can destroy the dark." My heart was beating against my chest with such a beat that it might have been producing its own symphony.

The runner faded away and I tensed, expecting blinding white light and a flash of blonde hair, but it wasn't a flash. It was a head flip and a sheet of blonde hair that I had seen one too many times.

Dread grew into an emotion so severe that I might as well be drowning in it.

I couldn't tell where she was, or when, but Ovailia stood in the middle of some cave, blood splattered over her face as her laugh twisted into fear and then the sight faded back to the tiny darkened room, the smell of dust and herbs that always filled the air so much stronger against the memory of fresh air I had been pulled from. Against all the questions that were now buzzing in my head.

"What the hell was that?" I snapped, the look on Ilyan's face telling me he had seen it all.

"You tell me, child." Dramin seemed more entertained than interested.

"Sight has never come to me like before," I said, staring between both Ilyan and Dramin who now sat before me, Ilyan in the old wooden thing that I normally sat on.

"That alone should tell you that your sight is not broken. It is not false or fragmented. As you wish, a little bit of training could be all that you need," Dramin said, fetching the still partially full mug from my hands and sipping on the remains. "Sight still comes to you. And perhaps we should assume that the sight is changing, and that you are not changing it. The fluidity of truth has always flowed like a waterfall, same as the magic of a Drak."

"Spoken like a true Drak," Ilyan teased, the two men chuckling with a sound that was too dark for my tastes. My mind was still spinning around it like a broken gear.

"But doesn't that mean the magic is broken, Uncle? If it's changing?"

"A change does not always equal a break. The wall today changed. It cracked, but it did not break. But you still learned something didn't you?"

My eyes widened, "Did you see that? I thought your sight was broken."

"Oh, it is," he said with a smile before taking another sip.

"Wynifred told me when she was here. There is always ways to gain information, always a new perspective to find. A new crack to break."

Dramin's eyes narrowed from over the top of his mug, his severe look digging into me as he took another drink and sat back against his pillows, letting his eyes sag as if he was going to sleep, as if Draks did much of that.

"I will teach you Joclyn," He whispered, "But you must no longer be scared of the secrets that are hidden inside your sight and inside this world. If I teach you, everything is going to come out."

I was suddenly regretting my choice to come here at all.

I looked at Ilyan, knowing full well that there was one sight I wasn't ready to part with, one that needed to stay in that dark forgotten cave where it belonged. Right beside Ovailia as she laughed like a mad man.

10

RYLAND

HIS VOICE RUMBLED in the back of my mind, but it was still there. It got worse the longer we were by the barrier. By the time we had seen the Vilỳs thundering through the air toward us it was a shout that I was struggling to ignore.

I couldn't get into the air fast enough.

By the time I landed outside of the castle complex it was back to a whisper, but I was going to need to blow off some steam to get rid of the madness completely.

I didn't like the out of control mania my father's voice gave me. It wasn't welcome.

"Ryland?" I whipped around at the timid question, unsurprised to see Risha dropping her shield right behind me. "Is it okay?"

I knew what she was asking and I had no interest in answering. Letting this woman, this beautiful, amazing woman that I was trying so hard to ignore my feelings for, into this shameful part of me was not something I was ready to do.

Not yet.

Perhaps not ever.

The people I let into my life have a tendency to get hurt, and I truly did not wish to do that to her.

Are you sure you have a choice in the matter? She is already in your life, she is sure to get hurt. Why not let it be at your hand?

"Yes... I mean no..." I stuttered more, nerves and madness battling for the top spot in my mind. "I'm fine."

My back tightened in a jerk and I strode away, into the invisible barrier of the wall Jos and Ilyan had placed around the cathedral. The magic had been refined since Joclyn first swathed the cathedral complex with it a little over a month ago. At first it had kept everyone in, and everything out. Now, thanks to Ilyan's added little sparks it only allowed those with the mark of his magic to pass through, in either direction. In addition to the lock on being able to speak or share where we were hiding, we were protected.

Didn't make getting past the barrier any easier. The moment I stepped into the shimmering white of the shield it felt as if I had been sucker punched by a dairy cow.

All the air was sucked from my chest, the pressure against my bones making everything feel as though I was being forced through a straw.

With no air in my lungs, and no hope of being able to draw an additional breath, my mind went into a panic, arms attempting to flail and grab at air, or lungs as if I might be able to force some of the stuff in there.

That would be, of course, if I could move.

The pressure was too much, the force of the magic too penetrating.

It didn't stop my mind from the panic, however, so, when I was flung out like a newborn babe my arms and legs instantly went into overdrive trying to accomplish every action I had sent to them into in the last few minutes.

I was barely able to keep my feet, a marked improvement from the first time when I did collapse onto the ground like a sprawling newborn.

I may be gasping and stumbling, but Risha stepped through as elegant and simply as if she was walking through a doorway.

"I will never understand how you can do that," I grumbled, attempting to straighten both hair and shirt in a bid not to look quite as crazed.

"It is not my first time dealing with Ilyan and his barriers." She was smoothing her shirt now, not that she needed it. It was perfect on her, and in the slightly red light of our camp brought out the flecks of blue in her hazel eyes.

I audibly sighed, that warm buzz being around Risha always brought me growing stronger. I was admiring her in a shirt, I wasn't sure how much longer I could avoid the pull of her. Or rather, how long I could convince myself that there wasn't a pull of her to ignore.

"It was a favorite of his back in the twelfth century when much of this began. It should have stayed there," she continued on, oblivious to the bright red blush that was spreading over my neck. Thanks to the dimmer red of the camp, it was much more noticeable than it had been beside the barrier.

"I am sure if we kick it hard it enough it can stream back from where it came from and get skewered by a knight or something." The idea seemed ridiculous, but Risha was nodding in agreement.

"Right through the chest, give it a taste of its own medicine." She snickered at her own joke, following me as I made my way toward the main area of camp and the main building where all the Chosen had been given rooms and training space.

I needed to fight some of this energy off, and that was the best place to do it.

The cathedral was fun to watch the Skřítek spar, or Joclyn and Wyn if you were lucky enough to find them there. The Chosen were still in training and far too unreliable to let them free in an ancient cathedral, however.

Or, that's what I would have to assume. I may not have known my brother long, but his love of churches and their cathedrals had preceded him years before my mother had been seduced by my father.

There was no way he was going to let them in there.

Which was fine, the less of an audience I had the better. Besides, the Chosen were always ready to spar with me. They didn't know my history. I wasn't a liability to them.

"I take it you are going to go battle away your demons by fighting a poor unsuspecting Chosen?" There was a bit of accusation in her voice, the hidden snap rolling over my back and I slowed my pace.

"They have to learn somehow and as much as I love Sain, I don't think his method is the right way to go."

"And you beating them up is?" She was clearly teasing, her brow knitting together as she rushed in front of me, holding her hand out as she pulled me to a stop.

"I'm not beating them up, Risha." Yes, I was, and I knew it, so did she. I half expected her to pop her hip with the look she was giving me. "They like it."

That part I knew was true. They never won, but just the idea of using their brand new magic against the king's baby brother was taking away the sting of all the bruises and gashes that I was giving them.

"Mmhmm." I tried to take a step forward, the voices were getting too loud and I needed to find an outlet before it got much worse. I didn't move so much as run into Risha's outstretched hand.

"I seem to recall you need permission to train the chosen now." Smug was a good look on her, her eyebrow peaked up in this perfect little arch...

Wouldn't you like to watch them furrow? To watch her scream?

I shook my head as if it would dislodge the voice. I need to get out of here. Battle. Needed. Now.

"I'm not training them. I am beating them up. As you put so eloquently." I tried to move past her hand, past the lithe fingers that were gently pressing against the layers of shirt, jacket, and scarves that I had put on after the fountain explosion. I was suddenly wishing I hadn't put on quite so many layers of clothing. She didn't move, and I didn't want her to.

"Why not beat me up instead?"

"Excuse me?" I knew what she said, but it wasn't computing quite right.

"Oh bother. Come with me." Risha wrapped her hand around mine, and pulled me away from the monastery and toward one of the far courtyards that had been set up for the more advanced training, but that hardly anyone had been using.

We may be under Ilyan's barrier, but for the Chosen and even some of the Skříteks the courtyard was too far away from the main camp to truly feel safe. I had more frightening things to be scared of, and Risha was walking so confidently that I wasn't sure if she was scared of anything.

She should be scared of you, Ryland. She should be scared of what I will do to her when I take control.

The possibility was almost too close to reality. With the Chosen I had to go easy so as not to accidentally kill them.

Going easy meant I could blow off steam and still keep control of my mind. Risha was at my skill level, she was perhaps even above it seeing as I was trained to fight dirty and kill.

I doubted her magic skill headed in that direction.

"Are you sure this is a good idea?" I was asking myself, but she answered, taking a quick step forward to turn around and face me as we walked, her back toward the opening that led to the courtyard.

"I guess that depends on what you think is a good idea," she smiled. "Not dying in a raid is a good idea. Not releasing tigers from the zoo is a good idea."

"Do we have plans to do that?" I asked, she ignored me and plowed through her list, shoes scraping against the grime covered street.

"Not accidentally turning your best friend into a ferret. Not letting your bastard father win is a--"

She didn't get to finish. A blast erupted right behind her, a bang echoing through the courtyard as an explosion erupted against stone and glass. It would be our luck that we would run right into an attack. Risha ran toward the blast, the smoke that was now drifting over the rooks the buildings looking like a call to war.

"This was so not what I had in mind," I groaned as I sprinted after Risha, a lifetime of Rugby training kicking in as I caught up and then overtook her, sprinting toward the courtyard at full speed, magic at the ready.

We didn't have to move as fast as we did. The supposed attack was nothing more than a little boy, his tiny frame looking like a speck among the massive empty square.

The kid wore clothes that were both too big and too small, the scavenged items stained and soiled by food, dirt, and what I was sure was blood. The blood made sense with how he was screaming, tears streaming down his face as different sparks of magic shot from his hands, the ill trained power was erupting nearly as violently as mine did when I lost control.

"Jaromir," Risha said as she caught up to me, pausing for half a breath before she charged into the courtyard.

This time it was my turn to hold her back.

"Let me," my voice was too hard as I strode passed her, bee lining for the kid who was still oblivious to our arrival.

He was still sending out attack after attack, letting the magic erupt into the air and against buildings as he sobbed.

I wanted an outlet, I wanted some danger to banish the voices, and nothing was better than sneaking up on an out of control little kid with untrained magic. Of course, in this instance I was more likely to be attacked first.

Shields up, I suppose.

Against a child? You are more pathetic than ever.

"Hey, kid." I spoke the second I was within earshot, doing my best to keep my tone positive. I'm not sure it mattered, the second I spoke, he turned with a shout, sending sparks of infantile magic right at me. The shield was hardly needed, I deflected the attack with little more than a snap.

That alone should shut my father's voice up.

Hardly.

"Hey there, I am not going to hurt you, and you certainly aren't in trouble" I said, the wrinkle in his nose was a telling sign that he didn't believe me. "We came to spar, too," I knocked my head back to Risha who was still standing in the entrance, waving enthusiastically. "Mind if we join you?"

Magic sparked between his fingers in what he thought was an ominous warning. I hadn't talked to Jaromir much since that first council after the attack, when Joclyn was welcomed as Queen.

After that, he was herded off to the bunks for the Chosen, and I went about my life as the king's partially deranged little brother.

The poor kid didn't seem to have fared as well as I had. He was unkempt, the clothes just the start to the messy hair, dirty face and broken shoes that he sported.

It wasn't just that, though, it was a dead light in his eyes that I swear hadn't been there before. It was a look I knew all too well. The look of loneliness. Of being forgotten.

My heart wrenched together, and I took another step forward, aware that Risha was approaching. He didn't seem to like either of our movements and sent up another spark of magic.

"Why are you here?" He asked, the words wrinkling the large Vilỳ kiss on his cheek and pulling his face awkwardly.

"To spar," Risha said, as bright as bubbly as always. "We'd love to join you, that was a good fire attack. I wasn't able to do one that good until I was much older. I'm impressed. Can you do an inverted flame?"

Jaromir's expression went from beaming pride to twisted confusion, his brow knitting together as he tried to figure out what she was talking about. I was just as confused as the kid, but only because that magic was advanced and something most people didn't learn for a few years, in some cases, hundreds of them. Risha, however, was smiling as if she was oblivious to what she had suggested.

"N...no?"

"I would love to show you," Risha answered, stepping toward him, and this time he did not step back. "Ryland knows a few tricks with fire magic. He's a pro."

There was the awed look I had seen in council, the shell shocked amazement over the world he had fallen into. I would take that over the concern of what was wrong with the kings' baby brother any day, and I would keep those facts about me hidden from him for as long as possible.

"Will you teach me? Please?" He asked, suddenly beaming, his eyes so wide that they were nearly all red from the light they were absorbing. "No one here will spar with me because I am a kid, and I don't know how to do anything. I come here because the older ones won't yell at me for being reckless. I mean, I haven't broken anything yet, but I did burn myself once. It was pretty cool to watch the skin heal."

Jaromir rambled as he twisted around to show us the faded scar on the back of his arm where he had allegedly burned himself. The scar was far too angry for your everyday magical accident, however. The kid was getting himself into dangerous territory, which could end badly without a little bit of help.

And you think you are the one to help him?

The voice was a sneering rumble, but even its attack could not eliminate the excitement that was growing inside of me.

Yes, I think I am the perfect person to help him. And do it the right way.

"Sure kid," I said, taking a step forward and shaking my hand through his hair like I had seen adult authority figures do on TV a few times. There was no starry eyed moment, however, just a wrinkled nose, a stare of disgust, and a twist to get away from my touch.

"I'd love to help you." I chose to ignore the whole incident and plowed on. "Risha and I know a bunch. We can get started now if you want."

Jaromir was back to beaming, but he wasn't the only one. Risha was smiling as though she had accomplished something amazing, the air buzzing with her magic as she stepped forward, preparing for lesson number one.

My eagerness for this had faded, but only because the second Risha's magic had flared, mine had reacted in a wave that had nothing to do with training, and everything to do with her.

Everyone around you gets hurt.

I didn't know if that warning came from the madness or from me, but I pushed it away, rushing toward Risha and promptly tripping over my own two feet, stumbling into her.

Unfortunately for me, she stepped to the side and I fell into the cobbles with a thud that echoed off the high walls of the old apartments.

"Maybe I will have you train me right now," Jaromir said between his giggles.

"I'm okay," I groaned, waving my arm behind me like it was a white flag. I was officially giving in.

Giving into falling. Probably giving into her.

Definitely giving into her.

11

SAIN

SHATTERING the ancient glass vase wasn't nearly as cathartic as destroying the tiny winged bats of Edmund's creation, but there wasn't much I could do about it right then. I couldn't leave the compound, not now. Not with the two of them locked up with my son.

"Bastard king!" I roared through the shattering of yet another vase, my frustrations ripping at the tattered wallpaper of my room, as if the words themselves were knives.

Shards of paper whipped into the air, spinning in the heat of my anger before they fell to the ground, right to my feet.

Not that they had anywhere else to go. Ilyan had assigned me what was the smallest room in the complex, the walls so thin that I could hear the Chosen argue next door, the infants not even skilled enough to cast a simple sound barrier between us. The floors were worn smooth, the glass in the pane cracked, and the walls peeling so intensely that I would often wake up with strips of the old floral pattern draped over my face.

Everything smelled of dust and the tiny bed barely fit, the iron frame wedged between the two walls so that it barely left room for a dresser, or the door to open all the way.

I deserved better.

Joclyn had clearly convinced him to punish me. Not that it would do much good, this was still nicer than the prison cell that Edmund had loved to keep me in. A tiny baby step toward my goal.

I wished it had more room for me to unleash my anger, and more objects for me to unleash my anger on, especially considering that I was trapped. There was no way of knowing when, or if, Ilyan would come check on me, and I needed to be ready to reach Dramin the moment they left.

Discover what they wanted, and be ready to repair any damage they had done.

I waved my hand over the shards of porcelain, forcing the scraps of glass back together as one so often does with bone. The cracks were still present, and the repair wasn't anywhere near permanent, but it would let me throw the thing again. I would get to watch it shatter against the cracking plaster.

And I could imagine all the other things that I wanted to crack with a vase and a bit of magic.

Pulling my hand back, I prepared to toss the vase into the plaster again, a certain person's smug little grin projecting itself onto the wall. Instead, the vase fell to the ground and shattered around my feet as a booming fist hit against the door three times and I jumped a few feet into the air.

"Damn it!" I roared, landing on the smooth floor, and the shards of porcelain atop it.

The porcelain acted like marbles, sliding between worn

rubber soles and smooth wood, sending me face first into the mattress again as the knock sounded once more. I suppose I had one reason to be grateful for a small room, I could have received a face of broken glass instead of stale blankets and a flat mattress.

"Who.. who is it?" I stuttered with false fear, even though my face was still furrowed in a scowl, eyes narrowed at the bits of glass as I hastily used my magic to sweep them under the bed.

"Zin." The voice on the other side of the door held as many nerves as mine, although I had a feeling that theirs were real. They were also completely unfamiliar, along with the name.

I had no idea who that was.

I closed my eyes, letting my magic drift through the air and through the door, opening up my mind's eye to see who was waiting. The same boy from the fountain stood, shaking, with five or six others. All of them were crammed into the hallways that was about the same size of my room, staring at the door with the same hope and wide-eyed wonder that I had seen in them when they waited around the entry to the hospital for Joclyn.

Except this time all of the eagerness was directed at my door, or rather me.

"Zin?" I made sure to keep the same amount of fear in my voice, sweeping the last of the porcelain under my bed as I tiptoed to the door, watching them in my mind and letting my magic drift closer, letting my power taste theirs.

Not that there was much there, they truly were untrained. And now they never would be if Ilyan had his way.

"The boy from the fountain, I had some... some

questions. Can I--?" I could practically hear him swallow from the other side of the door. "Can I come in?"

"And what of your friends?" I kept my eyes closed, their wonder deepening at the magic of my question. They really understood nothing. That skill was for babies. "Would they like to come in too?"

A girl with a particularly fuzzy braid of hair began tugging on Zin's sleeve, her eyes pleading with him to answer. What did she expect to happen? She had come all this way, after all. Surely, they had planned this out but no, Zin looked at the door, too stunned to know what to say. Thankfully, the girl spoke up, ready and willing to take things into her own hands.

"Yes, we would. Sain of the first. We would like to speak to you. To learn from you."

Oh, I liked this one.

Her eyes were earnest as she stepped closer to the door, her magic pricking up as she lifted her hand to the rough hewn wood, as if being that close was some kind of worshipful moment. She wasn't far from the truth.

I opened the door before her hand had a chance to make contact with the wood, the quick movement making her jump back, the awe in her grey-blue eyes expanding.

In fact, all of them looked as though their eyes had taken on the quality of American silver dollars. Two boys at the back were even mumbling and bowing toward me. It had been so long since I had seen that.

"You better come in quick," I pulled the girl in urgently, sure the others would run in after her and threw the door open as wide as it would go, which wasn't much seeing as the bed was in the way.

They all followed lead and thundered in as a herd.

Useful seeing as I wasn't supposed to be training or speaking to any of Joclyn's precious Chosen.

I can't help it if they come to me.

The door snapped shut the moment the last man entered, this one still bowing as he tried to figure out the correct way to greet me. I would have to show him the proper way.

The room was barely big enough for me, let alone the six others that had invaded, all of them looking around with differing states of confusion and awe.

"Please, please. Sit. Sit!" I pulled out the single folding chair, an old meditation pillow that had been left behind by the monks and sat myself down on the bed, looking right at the pretty brunette as I patted the hard mattress beside me. "Sit."

Her cheeks faded to the color of strawberries as she sunk down, careful to leave a bit of space between us. Normally I would say such an act was out of proprietary, but this girl was too star struck with me for that to be the case.

"What can I do for you?" They exchanged looks, most of them looking to Zin, who had lost his steam over being leader of the group. He sat, eyes wide, shoulders sagging, his jaw working as though the darn thing was broken.

I barely restrained my chuckle at the foolishness of it all.

"Surely you have sought me out for some reason?" I turned to the girl again, she seemed to be the only one among them with any amount of sense.

"We have." She didn't even hesitate. "It's about the fountain, and what happened with the Queen earlier today. She doesn't have the power you do. We want to know why."

I was liking this girl more and more. She was quick, quite nice to look at, and whether she knew it or not she pulled these six pathetic Chosen into a snare that I hadn't planned to set for a month at least. I guess the fountain had done its work better than I had assumed.

"Is there something wrong with her magic?"

"Yes," I sighed, dropped my shoulders and looked down into my lap, carefully winding my hands one over another in supposed agitation. "My poor daughter is troubled. So troubled."

My voice caught with a forced gasp, my shoulders sagging even more as I writhed my hands, staring at them even as I watched the faces of the others through my magic. Concern. Fear. The two men who were leaning against each other on the floor exchanged a look that could have made the air sing.

All of that washed from my mind as the girl placed her hand over mine, her touch soft, gentle, and without a drop of magic in it.

Pathetic.

"What has happened? Is there anything that we can do?" Her tone was calm and everything about her was tender and innocent. And so easily corruptible.

"Nothing that you can do, I am afraid." Her face fell as one of the others let out a low sigh.

"How about you?" one of the men on the floor asked. "Aren't you one of the first? Surly there is something you can do?"

"For my daughter?" I asked, perking up, although I did not pull away from the girl's hands. Magic or not, her touch was warm and somehow my power was reacting to it. I had a feeling that hers was a future I would like to peek into.

"The firsts' power stretches into the well of Imdalind, it is the strongest power there is among magic. I am the last one alive who possess it, all of my sisters and my brother have gone. Centuries ago." I gave a subtle head nod, my eyes downcast to where the girl had begun to run her finger over the back of my hand. "I doubt there is anything even I can do."

"Is that why she couldn't summon the water and the sight like you?" The girl asked again, her thumb freezing in place. "Because you are so powerful."

"Yes," I let the heat run under my skin right where she was touching me, letting it call to her magic. Unfortunately, I still felt nothing. From any of them. I was beginning to doubt that they had power at all. "Ilyan is powerful because of his parents. A child of a first of the Skříteks, and the first of all the Chosen Children. Joclyn pulls much of her strength from me, but with a mortal mother she can never reach her true potential."

I shook my head again and pulled away from the powerless grip of the girl, holding my hands in front of me as I produced a tiny orb of water. The dangerous poison splashed tiny droplets over the group, but none of them shied away, they all attempted to move closer, to see what was in my hands, and the perfect image of what I had meant to be Angela inside the orb.

But I hadn't produced an image of Joclyn's mother at all. Instead it was Ovailia, with her harsh eyes and perfect features. It seems my magic was trying to connect to hers more than I was aware.

This could spell trouble.

"That's amazing. Is that something only Drak's can do?" The older woman who had spoken from the back of the group wasn't even looking at me, she was staring at the image of Ovailia, reaching toward it as if to see if it was real.

I would rather she didn't, hers wasn't the future that I was interested in.

"No, anyone can do it," I said, letting the water drip back into my hand where it was safe. "Even you."

Shocked gasps and rumbling whispers broke through them, all of them scooting closer until the tiny space was beginning to feel claustrophobic. If I could scoot back I would have, but I was already inches from the wall, and trapped in place thanks to the army of lost dogs I had foolishly let into my quarters.

Oh dear, this close I was able to smell them a bit too well.

I needed their allegiance, yes, but I would like to be able to breathe while I earn it.

"Will you teach us?" The girl beside me asked, the subtle need I had felt for her fading away as the scent of her breath hit me full in the face.

"For the Well's sake, let me breathe."

As one, they realized what they had been doing and shifted away, most of them scuttling even further than they had been before, not that that meant much. The kid in the corner was back to bowing his head as he tried to figure out how to apologize. The girl next to him realized what he was doing and joined in, the two of them looking like broken bobble heads.

"Will you teach us?" The girl asked again, thankfully far enough away that I wasn't accosted by the foul odor of her breath.

They all leaned in again, although not as much as they had before. It was still enough to see the plea in their eyes, to feel the buzz of their hope. Hope that I should dash. I mean, I was forbidden from teaching the chosen.

In large groups.

I hardly counted these five as large, and Ilyan clearly didn't as well because I didn't feel a scrap of his binding magic trying to pull from answer. Not that I couldn't break it. Not that I hadn't planned to. I wouldn't let the man rule over me. The commands he made in anger were always the easiest ones to snap through. I would have to eventually.

But not today.

Later, when he knew what I was doing. When I could make him hurt for his attempt to lord over me. My soul was singing at that future,

I dragged my hesitation, grabbing my mug off the nightstand and filling it, causing the two that set beside me to shriek and shimmy in utter awe. I truly had no interest in training any of these fools in how to use their magic, and I had no intention of doing so. But I would give them knowledge, and I would love every minute of it.

If only because I knew I was defying Ilyan and his bride on every step.

"Of course I will," I said, taking a slow drink as they hollered in their victory. "What would you like to learn."

It was frighteningly obvious how little training the Chosen had been given that none of them had an answer. No request for a trick or a spell they had seen, no plea for a story or a history they may have missed. Just blank stares and side glances as they all waited for someone else to be brave enough to ask.

"Can you tell us what happened? With Prague and those *things*? They only tell us that Ilyan's father wants to destroy us, but we don't understand why."

I stared at the kid, his slightly upturned nose giving him an unfortunate look.

"Do you truly not know?" I leaned toward them, aghast, forcing more shock into my expression as they shook their heads in unison.

"They wouldn't even tell us that it was Ilyan's father. Zin overheard it one day. He speaks a bit of English, and we all know that the queen hasn't taken the time to learn our language." I hoped I wasn't imagining disgust in his voice. The twist of frustration was a beautiful harmony to the increasing pace of my heart.

"She was not born here unfortunately, she is still too young to know that her prideful choices can hurt those around her."

"I can tell." Even more disgust. Perfect. Perfect.

"What do you wish to know of Edmund?" I asked, taking another slow drink of Black Water while I waited for them to respond.

"What he did to us."

"And why?"

"So everything?" They all nodded their heads eagerly. How could I say no?

"I have been on this world since the beginning of magic. I have seen it all. I was there when all this started. I was the first to see." I leaned back, letting my mind wander to that first moment, to that first sight when I had shown Edmund the power he could have, and what was standing in his way.

When I had shown him what to do to destroy those who were in my way.

The beautiful images rumbled against my soul, my magic lifting through the last of the water in the mug, the power of Imdalind desperate to show them what was locked inside of me. To show them what I had seen.

They would never be worthy of that.

The story, however, I could give them.

"Ilyan was impatient in finding a woman to take as a mate and came to me begging that I find some girl that he could take as his own. This was before Edmund fell and Ilyan's lust was well known in the land. He took hundreds of girls to his bed in hopes of tricking their magic to bond with his. But he bored of that and forced me to give him sight, and what I saw has changed the course of history."

12

JOCLYN

Steam and dew clung to every surface in the tile bathroom I shared with Ilyan. The mirror was fogged over, the long subways tiles shimmered in the yellow vanity light, and the air hung with a fog that made the entire place that much more magical.

It was magical enough given that Ilyan had spoiled me with a rare shower, something that was much needed given the day I had.

For a few brief minutes, I had let the water hit over my face, my neck, and my back. I had let the scalding rain wash away every foul thought of my father and every fear that Dramin saw in me. Ilyan's touch had done a good job of helping that along, too. His fingers trailed in lingering lines over my face, my shoulders, dragging down the ridges of my spine and over my hips.

A shiver of pleasure and memory boiled against bone and muscle and I pulled the fluffy towel I had wrapped myself in a tad bit closer, breathing in the steam. Which didn't help at all, the steam was dripping with memories of touches and kisses that were like an electric firestorm inside my bones. And there I was, shivering again. A perilous action considering I was teetering on the edge of the bathtub, the ancient claw-footed thing not providing much in the way of sitting.

I needed to get my mind off the last hour or so that we had spent in the shower, but that also meant returning to the world of apocalyptic battles and bad guys. And that meant my mug.

It was sitting on the back of the toilet like some kind of award that you want everyone to see, but are only partially proud of.

I was sure that Ilyan had placed it there before he skittered off to grab something from our bedroom.

Presumably this mug.

The rough brown clay stood out against the white glistening tile like a pile of dog poo in a perfectly manicured lawn. Sain would be pissed if he heard me say that. I would have to log that away.

"I am quite sure I heard Wyn warn you against some kind of wrinkled potato scowl earlier today," Ilyan's light mocking drifted through the steam as he stepped back into the room, closing the door with a faint snap and sending the last of the steam swirling in ribbons of white, grey, and blond hair.

He stood, with his own fluffy white towel clinging to his hips, the fabric pulling against the low ridges of his bones and accentuating the deep lines of muscle that made up his abs, his hips, his... I swallowed and looked back to the mug, if only to keep my hands off him. He looked better without the towel.

He looked good with the towel too.

He just looked good.

Darn it all, I was totally in love with him.

'I'm in love with you too, Můj kamarád,' His whisper burned inside my mind as he stepped toward me, the light tap of his feet pulling my attention. I stubbornly continued to look at the mug, however, even when his fingers twisted through the wet strands of my hair. *'Even when you scowl so much you end up looking like a wrinkled potato.'*

"I do not look like an old wrinkled potato, Ilyan," I said with too much gusto, my wet hair whipping through the air as I turned to him, his blue eyes now inches from mine, the lines of gold picking up every bit of light that reflected off the white tiles.

"I wouldn't care if you did." His breath was cold against my skin, thanks in part to the boiling need that was surely heating me into a furnace. The hot and cold was a firestorm, and I shivered, which caused Ilyan to smile and the whole world to start spinning as I leaned in and kissed him.

I couldn't control myself. The light in his eyes was infectious, the swell of his magic inside of me was an anchor that I couldn't swim away from if I tried.

And I sure wasn't trying.

I let my tongue drag against his, my teeth pull against his bottom lip until he groaned and pulled me into him, his hand flat against my back. Just his touch and I could tell we were going right back into steamy shower-time.

Which would be fine, if that mug wasn't staring me right in the face like some kind of curious toddler. Okay, that analogy was worrisome and something I was so not ready for.

"You could always look away," Ilyan breathed into my ear, trying to pull my focus as he kissed the skin beside my mark, turning the fireworks up to a solid twenty.

Now we really were playing with fire.

"Your wife, the wrinkled potato," I breathed, doing

everything I could to steady myself as I pulled away from him, although his hand only dropped to my hip.

"You put that there, didn't you?" I asked, his face turning up into a guilty smile as he pulled the question out of my mind.

"Yes, but not for the reason you think. We had spent an hour in the shower. Together. That's a lot of energy. I am sure you need food. I need food. It was not my intention to bring back the same thoughts from before."

"Dramin was right."

"About the shower?"

Gross.

The look I gave him moved me firmly into wrinkled potato status.

"No, he was right that I am scared. But I'm not scared of sight. I'm scared of the future. I'm scared of seeing something that I don't wish to become real."

"So.... sight." He prodded my hip lightly, his fingers trailing down my thigh and over my knee before he stood.

"No." Although yes, because what I had explained was clearly sight. "I'm afraid that Sain is right. That things are broken, that what I am seeing is some kind of prophecy and I can't change them. Even though we have changed a few things, and that my magic wanted me to change those things."

"The world hasn't exploded yet," Ilyan said as he grabbed the mug, his hand wrapped around the thing as he passed it to me.

He was pretty much the only person who wasn't terrified of the thing. Everyone else treated the mug like poison, even though it was just the water that was on the danger scale.

"That all depends on who you would ask, Ilyan. I mean we are sitting inside a red dome."

"I was under the impression that we are sitting in a bathroom, you and I. No one else is here." He nodded toward the mug, and for the first time in a while I wasn't sure I wanted to drink. The whole instant sight from Dramin's room was sitting too heavy.

"No one else matters," He whispered into my ear, leaning into me until his warmth wrapped around me like a blanket, his chest pressed against my shoulder, the soft ridge of one of his scars burning against me.

He was covered with them, the scars of black water that had brought him sight of me, and me of him. I sighed and resisted the urge to trace the crisscrossed lines of his chest and instead covered the mug with my palm, the old clay heating against my skin.

"Do not hold stock in what your father says, my love. Follow your magic, follow your sight, it hasn't failed you yet."

I nearly dropped the mug, he didn't know what he was saying. He didn't know what I had seen. His death. My death. The entire world cracking open like an egg, if you would believe Sain.

I was sure that the whole world couldn't crack open like an egg. It didn't matter. I wasn't going to let that happen. I was determined, and I think that was what I was scared of. That was the bit that Dramin was warning me about, whether he had seen it or not.

I was scared of whatever Sain was hiding. I was scared of the futures that I couldn't change as much as the ones I could. Holding all this future in my head was daunting, especially with my father hissing about how wrong it all was that I couldn't change it.

But I had changed it, I had practically heard my magic whisper to me like some kind of cricket guide, and it wasn't saying anything about how everything was carved into stone by a god, well unless that god was Sain. It said to heal Dramin. It said I could save Ilyan.

My brother had said I must not be scared of the secrets that are hidden in my sight. That didn't say anything about being scared of the future. Or being scared of my father. He said there were secrets, and if that cricket sized whisper was any hint I would say that was what I was scared of.

Sain was 'the first of his kind', but the only thing I knew for sure about him was that he was lying.

I sighed and chugged the liquid gold that I had conjured into my mug, the warm and spicy Black Water feeling like a balm against my heart, all warm and pleasant and healing. If my heart had been stabbed by my so-called father, all of those marks were soothed away, pulled into nothing.

Smacking my lips like a child with a sucker, I set the mug back in my lap and turned to Ilyan who was looking at me so intently I was almost sure I had turned into a wrinkled potato. I don't think I had ever seen so much vulnerable curiosity on his face before, the look was so unlike him that I may have laughed too riotously.

"No sight, and no potato either," I whispered, letting my hand cup his jaw before I brushed my lips against his, the touch wiping away the affronted scowl that had taken over his curiosity. "But thank you for my mug."

I smiled brightly, lifting the mug to eye level as if I was toasting him. He didn't even notice with how he was staring at me, the gleaming lines of gold swallowed by the look of pride that always followed me around.

"Don't be afraid of what it holds, my Joclyn. Don't be afraid of your power. It is stronger than your father's. I know this. You know this." Ilyan's eyes had locked mine in a stranglehold as he pulled the mug between us. He didn't even look away as he placed my palm over the ridge of the mug, the powerful awe in his eyes swelling so that I was looking at the king, and not just my mate.

"Call the water to you again." I never liked when he commanded me, but this one had an especially low growl in it, the tone pulling at me like a deliciously feral animal. I tried to pull away from the mug, but he kept my hand there, his thumb tracing the lines between my thumb and forefinger.

"I don't think this is a good idea." I hated that my magic was rising to press against the wall of power that his ability had bathed the bathroom in. My Drak magic was pulling strong against my heart.

This was not going to end well.

"Trust me, my love." Thank god the deep furrow of power had left his voice, although it wasn't making the situation any better. He was still looking at me with all the strength of the ruler I had seen drive that car more than a year ago. A girl with a broken back, and a king that destroyed an army.

I did my part too. But still.

The look was a whole other level of hot.

"Fill the mug."

I screwed up my face as I did so, pushing a few choice profanities into his mind, but he only chuckled. His other hand wrapped around my waist, pulling me into him until our hips touched, the two of us balanced on the edge of the tub as though it was the edge of a knife, a cup of poison precariously perched between us.

"Close your eyes," he said, the slight tremble in his voice giving him away.

I could see what he was planning a moment before he did it. I couldn't even inhale, let alone stop him before he dipped the tip of his already burned finger into the mug and my magic connected with the water, and with him, and pulled me right to the place that I did not want to be.

My vision went red as he screamed with the burn, my magic spiked, and the sound of water, fire, and Ilyan's pain flooded my ears. Ilyan's scream of pain threatened to rip my heart in two, but not as much as the image of the cave that I was assaulted with.

It was the same blood, the same limp and dead hand. I tried to block him from the sight, to block him from whatever was happening, but the magic was pulsing with the power of a title wave. The air around me was pulsing with it, right alongside the rampaging twist of my heart.

"The blood will flow before the end." The deep voice of sight poured from me, it bounced off the tile and mixed with the sounds of waves and fire that were echoing in my ears for some odd reason.

I couldn't focus on that, however, because the sight was changing, it was shifting past what I had seen before. The hand, the blood, it was painfully familiar. Before it showed the lifeless eyes of my mate, the vision shifted to a pulsing light surrounded by white tiles, and then to a blood streaked cement wall. Or perhaps it was a floor, nothing about it made sense.

Before I could get a good look, my mind was filled with beeping and flashing green lights similar to what I had seen in the hospital, back when I had been bitten. Back before my father had left. Back when I was normal and human. Except that was wrong. I was never normal and human, I had always been the daughter of a Drak.

"The end will echo the past, it will give birth to the future." The words made even less sense than the last riddle my Drak blood had poured out. Well, except for the past.

Before the vision faded to black, I got one clear look at a heart rate monitor and a bit of bushy brown hair that I wasn't sure I recognized. My mother maybe? I know she hadn't left my side while I was in a coma. Although, I don't remember her hair being quite so frizzy.

It didn't matter, the sight was gone before I could get a good look, and I opened my eyes to an ecstatic, and very wet, Ilyan. Water was dripping through the long strands of his hair, dripping off his nose and trailing over his chest in ripples of wet. Even his towel was soaked.

"Was I gone so long you decided to take another shower?" I asked, fully aware that he was placed against me exactly how he was before, his hips still smashing into mine.

"No." His lips twitched into a smile as his hand left mine, his palm pressing against my cheek, the freshly burned finger glistening with the poison of Black Water. "Just watching my amazing queen."

He didn't say more before his memories plunged into my mind, although these weren't the thoughts or images of years ago. It was a few minutes ago, when the bathtub filled with water and towered over us, showing him everything I was seeing. As Sain had done.

No. As the Draks did. Draks like me.

My father could do his own thing, I was just me, and it was just my magic. And if my magic told me I could save the world with a flash dance I was going to do it.

"Make it a tango," Ilyan whispered as he leaned into me, the pride in his eyes burning so strong I could feel the warmth wrap around me. Although, that could have been his hands as he held me against him, and his fingers as they trailed over my spine with a shiver that reached all the way to my toes.

"You know I have a wicked tango."

13

RYLAND

I HATED BEING in the city. I hated the smells and the way death and danger clung to every corner. But most of all, I hated how the buzzing and panic in my mind pricked up against the back of my neck like a fly that I couldn't swat away.

Normally, Ilyan would keep my expeditions to one a week, any more than that was pushing it, and here we were. Pushing it.

Joclyn had fallen asleep shortly after our failed attempt to puncture the barrier two days ago, and had been sleeping ever since thanks to some weird Drak thing that I didn't understand. Ilyan had requested to stay with her, although the way he glared at Sain when he said it made me think the choice had more to do with the old man.

I wish the two of them would get over whatever vendetta they had against Sain and leave him be. He had saved my life. He had saved Wyn's. He had done everything in his power to save Thom. He was clearly on our side. I hoped that they could see that before all this was over, because their pettiness was putting me in danger.

Not a danger from yourself, surely. Don't you mean danger for everyone around you. They know what is inside of you. They know to fear you.

I wasn't going to give the voices the satisfaction of looking. I knew that the Skříteks and the few advanced Chosen that had been assigned to me and this mission were fixing me with glares that belonged in the 'Museum of the Side Eye'. They always did, it was something I had become used to.

Look back, Ryland. Give them what they expect. Give them the show they came to see.

Shaking my head wasn't enough to dislodge the malice in his laugh, but I did it anyway. At least this time we don't have to go quite as close to the edge of the barrier. We avoided the small shops and stores closest to the castle Complex so as to not leave hints as to our location to Edmund and his men, but in this case that meant going across the river to a small shopping district in the new town.

The big box store was an eyesore in a city this ancient, but now it had a purpose beyond the gaudy.

I held up my hand in a fist, pulling everyone to a stop before signaling to the alley beside us, the narrow roadway looming with an inky darkness thanks to the height of the buildings on either side. Shuffling feet and the rustle of jackets and bags were far too loud in the quiet of the abandoned city, but thankfully we hadn't come in contact with any of the flying beasts yet.

We needed to get in, get supplies, and high tail it back to the complex.

You know they won't attack you, Ryland. You are my son.

I was thoroughly refusing to accept both the title and the voice right then.

"Everything good so far." Risha hissed as I followed them

into the alley. Her half statement, half question was a bit too knowledgeable. It was nothing more than a twitch, but of course she had seen.

"Peachy." I tried and failed to keep the growl out of my voice, I didn't need any of them picking up on the nuances of the conversation.

The Skřítek closest to us was still giving me the same look they had when Risha had escorted them to the tiny courtyard we used as an entry and exit point. I had watched the pride at having been chosen by the king for an expedition fade into an extreme distaste and malice at being chosen for a mission that was being led by the king's messed up baby brother.

"Can we get this over with?" I asked, shifting the straps of the burlap bag on my shoulder, as if the empty thing needed shifting. I had been using it for a little over a month and the thing was already threadbare and ripping in places. I could ball it up and put it in my pocket if I needed to.

I would if we weren't so close to the strip mall. Food and clothes were an alley away, and the easier I could grab the stuff on my list, the quicker we could get back.

"Impatient, your majesty?" Risha was kidding, but the glaring Skřítek furrowed his brow and scuttled toward the end of the alley with the rest of them, their round faces peeking around the end of the buildings to get a good look at our destination.

"No, I would just rather not call too many Vilỳ to us before we get there." I nodded toward the group, their whispering picking up in volume even from here. If their big white eyes weren't a beacon for the flying rats, that would be.

"Of all the cotton hauling mustard ninnies..." A string of the weirdest array of words followed her as she charged to the group, her face screwed up dangerously as she pulled the five of them back from the edge of the building, finger waggling, the hissing reprimand clear.

It was times like these I was glad I spoke fluent Czech. She sure was cute when she was mad.

Ugh. Now was not the time to be having thoughts like this.

Why, son? Are you still thinking you can protect her somehow? You know it's too late.

My heart cringed, but I wouldn't let the emotion show on my face. I pushed the straps of the bag up a little higher and took two steps toward the others. The second I got within ear shot, the volume of her reprimand picked up. A warm wave moved over me as I walked through the shield she had erected to block sound so that she could ream into the morons.

Risha was very quickly becoming one of my favorite people. Darn it. No. Yes.

This was so not the time to be having thoughts like that. Now I should be thinking about battling my father's monsters and keeping all these people safe. I should not be thinking about how her hair looks in the dark, the way she takes charge...

My heart somehow managed to simultaneously pick up and drop to my toes at the thought, that blush that I had been trying to keep at bay the other day covering me as quickly and as effectively as her shield.

"You follow me, you follow your prince. You go one toe out of line and you will get us all killed," she spoke in quick Czech, the timber and rough edge of both words and voice sending those same smug Skříteks into a cower.

And there my heart went again, doing its drop to my toes tango. I needed to put some space, and perhaps some air that wasn't perfumed with the aroma of death between us.

"It's time to kiss this girl," I was trying to sound as powerful and in control as her, and it would have worked too. If it wasn't for what I had said.

Risha's tirade stopped, and all six pairs of eyes turned to me, differing levels of confusion and worry plaguing each furrowed brow. Great. As if I needed more reason for all of Ilyan's men to think I had a screw loose.

Surely you don't think it is just the one?

"I mean, we need to blush." More stares, and more thundering dancing from my twisting heart. I was starting to wish both this conversation and this situation had an eject button.

"Let's go," I said each word slowly, letting my nostrils flare as I took what should have been a cleansing breath. That was not possible here. I either inhaled rot or the smell of her perfume. I got a bit of both and the combination was doing weird things to my brain.

I strode past them, through Risha's barrier and right to the edge of the alley, pulling a shield over me as I peered from around the buildings. Checking for signs of Vilý, Edmund's men, or both.

The large thoroughfare that separated the alley from the store was a danger zone and required each of us to conjure an individual shield, which meant it was easier to get separated and easier for whatever might be waiting to pick us off one by one.

It had happened before, and I didn't have Ilyan's skill of forcing these guys to follow me.

My shield slid away as I turned back to the group, the same looks of frustration and worry they had before peering back at me.

"Everything is clear," I said from behind clenched teeth. I was determined not to let their distrust affect me, and I was already failing. "You will each need to shield yourselves and head toward the door under the large picture of the girl with glasses. Stay alert, stay vigilant, and only enter the door once I have opened it. Give me one click so I can get a count and make sure we don't lose anyone."

No one nodded, no one agreed, and I really didn't care. I gave Risha one tight lipped stare and she nodded, twisting back to them and basically repeating the same thing I had said. This time they nodded, agreed, and even asked a question. You would think I was speaking gibberish with how they responded, but I grew up speaking Czech the same as the rest of them.

Perhaps you should teach them how to respect you, Ryland. All it takes is a little bit of blood.

"We need to move," I growled again, my shoulders a tight line as I interrupted Risha and dropped my shield back over myself, taking off into the courtyard without another word. I would have to trust Risha to get them in position and moving, there was a reason she always took up the rear of these darn things.

Back in my past life, Joclyn and I would sit in my room for hours, eating candy bars, watching grade B movies, and playing video games. While she had a soft spot for racing games, I loved the first person shooters. I loved the archaicness of using a gun instead of magic. I loved the tactical way of fighting and stalking your prey. This courtyard, this forgotten city painted with a red tinted sun reminded me of those games. My hands ached for a gun, even though the magic that flowed through my veins was substantially more powerful.

Turning on the balls of my feet, I swept myself over the

courtyard, peering from rooftop to darkened alley, to each pile of rubbish and destroyed car in search of man or beast that would attack us. In the red light of the dome everything was too frightening. Every shadow turned into a Trpaslík in my mind, and I was sure that I was hearing wings.

Wings that were everywhere.

The buzzing mixed with laughter until I couldn't differentiate between what was my madness and what was the nasty Skříteks my brother had sent with us. The sounds grew louder, the shadows grew closer, and my heart was pulling so tightly in my chest that it was clear the madness would win this time.

I knew it was too soon for me to come back out here.

And then I smelled her perfume. The subtle aroma of lavender, sandalwood and what I was sure was rose drifted over me, wrapping around my heart and calming the darn muscle enough that what I had sworn was wings faded to the sound of sneakers against stone, and the shadows didn't seem quite so frightening.

The world was still dangerous, but right then it didn't seem so bad.

You truly are a fool if you believe a woman can change so much. They are good for nothing more than the magic the carry.

I threw open the door, the well-oiled hinges not making so much as a pop as one after another they entered with a click of their tongue and dropped their shield, Risha's shield the last one to drop before the door pulled shut.

"Get what you have been assigned," Risha instructed when there was still a sliver of red light against the floor. "Keep your shields up and move fast and silent. The place is full of dangers. You have ten minutes, and ten minutes only. We will leave without you. We have before."

Everyone nodded before their shields snapped back into

place, dropping them all from sight and leaving Risha and I to pause, for her to give me one long look that my mind and heart put way too much emotion and meaning behind. Was she worried, proud, confident? Did she like me?

Why were women so complicated?

And why was I thinking about this now in the middle an apocalyptic reconnaissance mission?

"You'll be okay," she whispered before pulling her shield over her, leaving me standing near the door with my still empty canvas bag over my shoulder.

I truly wanted to believe her.

You would be a fool if you did.

Then I must be a fool because I was totally believing her. If only for the matter of stubborn spite.

I went right to work, running a few feet away from the door where the shoes had been kept and to the display of sneakers that was slowly getting picked clean. Opening my bag, I carefully checked my list and began shoving shoes and as many socks as I could into the worn and frayed fabric.

Size thirty-two, twenty, child's sized thirteen. They were all here, even the pair of size adult forty-ones that I was trying to stuff into the bag when the whole thing ripped and sent shoes, socks, the few other trinkets I picked up scattering over the ground, over a display and into an old mannequin that promptly fell over with a noise loud enough to wake the dead, or rather every single Vilỳ in the place.

Which is exactly what happened as the department store filled with screeches and howls of the beasts. All of them heading right towards me.

I swore. Loud. After all, what did it matter anymore? Looking around for another bag I grabbed at the purses and bags at a nearby display, trying to find something big enough and not sealed with a security device. I was already causing way too much noise. I doubt the beasts could hear much over their screams to get to me if I moved fast enough.

I needed to find a bag. Another display fell over and I grabbed at the closest thing, an old faded backpack that looked more worn than a new bag should. It wasn't new, it was full of clothes. I swapped out the contents with the shoes as fast I could and high tailed it to the door, unsurprised to see it open.

At least they had enough sense to get out of here.

They had, however, not escaped without notice.

The door was open, the Vilỳ that had been chasing me were streaming out and into the courtyard where the flashes of magical attacks were blasting through the filthy glass of the door like gun fire.

Red. Blue. Purple. Everything sparked with color as if a fireworks display was happening outside. A show full of screams, grunts, and the smell of blood. One of those shouts I recognized. I had sparred with her enough lately to know it.

The bag was secured over my back and I was bolting out the door before I could think better of it. I would rip every single one of those little bastards out of the air if I needed to. My magic was swelling in my fingertips as I burst from the door and to what I had assumed was a Vilỳ massacre.

But the things didn't even seem to notice.

They flew past me, through the door, the smell of rot nauseating as their wings hit against my back and shoulders and the creatures took to the sky, soaring away from the battle before them, and the cloaked figure that stood fighting in the center.

One of the Skříteks was already down, the Chosen who

had been permitted to come along had taken shelter behind an abandoned car and was rocking and crying as he curled in on himself, as if he could make himself small enough that no one would notice him.

Risha and two of the Skříteks fought against the cloaked figure, their hands moving quick as the figure spun between the three of them, blocking every attack, and doling out enough of their own magic that Risha and the others were having trouble keeping up. The figure's magic did not drip like Edmund's men, it did not glitter with that bit of gold that most Skříteks did, and it did not have that same rumble in the air as the Trpaslíks.

I had never felt anything like it. I had never seen anything like it. I wasn't even sure what I was looking at. The figure's cloak was pulled so low over their face that I wasn't sure if we were fighting man or woman. I couldn't possibly tell whose side they were on.

But they certainly weren't on ours. Risha was trying to reason with them, but it was as if they couldn't hear. The attacks kept coming.

The Skřítek who had shown me so much disdain before, jumped away from one attack, only to be hit with a brilliant lavender light that filled the courtyard and reflected off the broken glass of the buildings as he was lifted into the air and dropped like a pile of bricks.

The man didn't move.

And something in me snapped. Like me or not, I couldn't let them go down like this. Especially Risha.

The backpack thumped against my back as I secured my shield, making sure that I was hidden from view and that my magic was locked in my heart as I had been taught so many times before. I didn't know what the attacker's power was, but I wasn't going to give him any upper hand.

The figure's cloak fanned behind them like a cape as they spun, a stream of magic flowing away from them and right to the three that were still fighting. Risha was able to dodge the attack, but the others weren't quite so lucky. Their arms and legs flailed through the sparks of magic as they arced through the air, hitting hard against road and walkway before collapsing back against the ground.

"You don't have to do this," Risha was continuing to plea with the figure, her petition pulling their focus enough that I was able to slip past her and to the attacker without notice. That was until I tried to reach out and place my hand against his shoulder, my magic ready to take him down.

The gnarled hand of the cloaked figure wrapped around my wrist, with the strength I wouldn't expect from a hand so mangled. A darkness pressed against my skin from their touch, a heat growing through my veins before a single attack pressed right against my heart with a zap that broke my shield and burst me back into the world with a pop and a scream. It took all my strength to stay standing, something which they hadn't expected.

I may still be haunted by my father's voice, but it was also my father's voice that pulled through me now, years of his torturous training snapping into place. Years of broken bones, or being forced to fight. To kill.

I couldn't help it, I smiled. I smiled and let a fan of magic pull from my hand and into the concealed face of the attacker.

"Ryland, no!" Risha screamed from somewhere behind me, her panic nearly pulling my focus.

Nearly.

The attack hit with a spray of blood, the cloaked man shuffling back with a howl that could have been either masculine or feminine. I had never heard a sound like it before, and it chilled my bones as though I had been plunged in ice. Even Risha stepped back at the sound, a genuine fear widening in her eyes as she tried to signal me away, begging me to soar away, to escape.

I wasn't about to leave her and the others here.

I moved to attack again, swinging my hand, but the attack was stopped by one of theirs, a bright flash of grey that sliced against my face as their hand slammed into my rib cage, another spark of magic moving into me and cracking a few ribs. I wanted to scream at the pain that was twisting over my chest, at the scarlet warmth that was trickling down my face.

Instead, I laughed. I had experienced worse.

The deep chuckle forced the hooded figure to step back and I attacked again, another spark of magic right to the face, perfectly placed to knock the hood right off their ugly mug.

I missed, although barely, the fabric had shifted to reveal a tuft of brown hair and an ear.

Trained to slap cloaked villains. You can do better than that.

I can, Father. Isn't this what you wanted.

Isn't this what you trained me for?

To kill.

"Kill." The madness took control and I stepped closer, another attack barreling toward the figure as they desperately tried to re-affix their hood.

It looked like they didn't want us knowing who they were. I could remedy that. Either by hood or life removal. Either way, I would get what I wanted.

I slammed my hand forward, my father's laugh echoing in my ears as an attack ripped through the air, sparking white and yellow against the red world and coloring the sides of the buildings as though they had been hit by the sun. The attack only made it halfway before the figure shot it down, his wrinkled hand swiping it away as he sent his own attack.

I dodged it lithely, hitting him with two more sparks of magic, one right after the other as I jumped into the air, magic and madness hurtling me toward the figure who sent one attack, straight into my face and chest.

This time I screamed.

Bones ripped from my body, skin split in a burning agony that I had only felt a few times before. My magic fell away as I hurtled past where they had been standing, heading right toward the bench behind. I had seconds to act, my magic only barely able to catch me before I kissed metal, cement, and a serious head injury.

Twisting in the air, I sent one quick attack into his back, immobilizing him as I kicked off from the bench that would have made a terrible headrest and changed my path. Right to the back of the creature who had turned away in supposed victory.

One arm wrapped around the attacker in a move I had mastered with far too many years of rugby. The other hand slammed into his back and into the coarse material of the cloak as I sent a bright spark of power into his spine. The magic was meant not only to immobilize, but to track and to spark against their magic so that I would know exactly what I was facing.

But nothing came back to me. No spark. No warning. It was as if their magic wasn't there, even though I could see a faint shadow of green against the street as they prepared to counter.

"Oh no you don't," I snapped, attacking them again, this time with a heat that sent the figure howling, their legs buckling as they dropped their weight.

I tightened my arm against them, holding them up without much effort. Another thing that rugby was good for. With my arm around his neck and my hand against his back, there was no way this guy was getting away now.

"Tell me who you are! Who do you work for?"

I held on tighter, tightening my arm over his neck as I pulled, desperate to cut off their air supply and incapacitate them enough that I could reach the hood, that I could identify them. That I could capture them.

I had only begun to reach for the hood when a brilliant flash of green spread over us, the light growing as if it was bursting out of the cloaked figure, blinding the world. I tightened my grip, cringing against the light as it burned my eyes until the back of my skull was catching fire. Everything felt as though it was burning, as though it was about to explode.

A scream of agony ripped through my throat, pulled from the pain as I gripped the figure tighter only to find that he was gone, the light having left with him. It was only me, standing in the middle of the courtyard, clinging to myself as I screamed in agony.

I didn't need the voice of my father to cement my own madness.

The look that the Skříteks gave me as they pulled themselves to their feet, however, told a different story.

The disappointment had gone. There was only awe as they stared at me, as I stood in a pool of blood, the crimson fluid dripping from my fingers.

Are you sure it's not fear?

That time I was sure.

14

JOCLYN

THE LAST THING I remembered was drifting off into utter bliss, the hot sun on my back, the sand in my hair, wrapped in nothing but fluffy towels and Ilyan. After that there was a brief moment of dusty sheets, red sun and the scent of shower before I drifted off to sleep. This time on a mattress that was too hard, but still wrapped in nothing but towels and Ilyan.

Watching Wyn run down a ruined street in the middle Prague, wearing a cloak she swore she didn't own hadn't been anywhere on that itinerary. Especially when everything felt too real, and too much like I was there and not dreaming.

I'd had dreams of sights before, but they had been oddly distorted, mostly involving Ilyan's dead hand and twisted by my subconscious into a nightmare that tried to rival the horrors of Cail's mind. Luckily, I had lived through those horrors and any reanimated sight nightmares did little more than wake me up with a gasp. No screaming, I doubt there was even a drop of sweat.

This was not like those nightmares.

In fact, if I had to guess I would say that this was real. That I was really watching Wyn run down a street in Prague. That she really was scared enough that her pupils were shaking, that her mouth was open in a scream she couldn't force to come. I had never seen Wyn look scared. Ever. Even when we were in the forest around Rioseco, surrounded by Edmund's men and certain doom, she was ready to kick some butt. There wasn't a drop of fear then. Now there was. The look on her face alone was enough to turn this into a nightmare.

Nightmare Wyn looked back at me again, her eyes wide in horror before she turned away, a sound that I could have sworn was a laugh drifting behind her as she pulled the hood up, the heavy fabric dropping her face into shadow.

The laugh picked up and so did my heart rate, the pulse so loud I could hear it my ears, even though this was only a dream. It was a dream, wasn't it?

"Wyn!" I tried to yell after her, to stop her, to do something. But the word was stuck in my head. She kept running, turning one corner and then another, before she looked back again. Although this time it wasn't Wyn.

Ryland was staring at me from underneath the hood.

Ryland with his black eyes and twisted smile that scared me more than any nightmare. More than any sight. That scream I had seen on Wyn's face before ripped through my mind, my feet stumbling back in an attempt to get away.

Except I didn't move back and he didn't stop his run to chase me. He smiled at me with all the nefarious malice that had plagued him for so long and continued running, the same laugh from before lifting in volume.

He hadn't even turned. Had he seen me? Black eyes meant danger for him, and yet he continued forward, and I followed him like a fool. A fool that had no feet to follow, just like I had no feet to stumble away from him.

Ryland looked back again, his eyes dark, his smile as much of a twisted horror against my spine. I could feel the panic, even though I didn't slow. Even though Ryland wasn't looking at me. He was looking at something behind me. Something far away.

He didn't even see me.

Because I wasn't there.

I was no longer sure if this was simply a nightmare.

He resecured the hood as he turned a corner, everything about him shrouded by the black cape, by the darkness of night and the deep scarlet shadows that drifted between the buildings as the last of the sun dipped behind the horizon and left us in our eternal sunset. This wasn't even now.

This was just as I had seen before, in the cathedral. Wyn and her cloak. Now Ryland and his cloak.

Sight.

But Sight while sleeping, that wasn't a thing as far as I knew. Perhaps Ilyan and I had gone too crazy with our bathtub experiments of the night before and now my subconscious was taking a joyride. Or the day before. Who knows how long I had been asleep for. I was a Drak, it could be days at this point.

Either way, my magic was humming through my veins and I was dreaming in sight. Well, I was, before the figure that I was following turned again and this time both Ryland and Wyn had left, replaced by my father and a look I had never seen on his face before.

He had all the power of Wyn right before she was going to kick some butt, and all the deranged darkness of Ryland, with just a dash of fear. At least I think it was fear, there was only a few things that could make a jaw tense like that, make the vein in his neck pop. Fear, or me.

I was going to go with fear if only because I had never seen such strength in him. He was unrecognizable. He was frightening. His eyes narrowed in a warning I didn't understand before he turned away, darting between two buildings and into a tiny alley, leaving me to follow him as we got closer and closer to the barrier.

It took me a second to recognize right where he was going. The tree from the courtyard was a silhouette between buildings, but it was there. Wyn and I were crouched beside the wall, peering through it in our search of autumn leaves and zombie cows.

I knew this moment, I had been here.

I mean I was there. Right there, in this weird sight dream.

Sain darted around another building, changing his trajectory as he raced toward the wall only stopping when he reached another small courtyard that had been cut in half by the barrier. The trees, the benches, everything about it was identical to the one that we had cracked the barrier in. Everything was the same, except we weren't in it, and there was no sign of Wyn's weird battle igloo.

The cloaked figure came to a stop, the vision stuttering behind them before the figure turned. I expected Thom, or Dramin, or anyone else to be beneath the dark tattered fabric, but it was still Sain. Sain and a twisted smile that was turning this whole thing into a nightmare equal to Cail and his twisted mind.

This time I stepped back, the image following my command as the single tap of a shoe against stone rang through the silence, the gentle clink like the bang of a gun in my ears, the sound instantly followed by the scream of the Vilỳ and a flood of wings.

They were coming. They were right behind him. There were thousands of them and they were heading right for us. We needed to run, but he didn't even flinch, the same look of power pulsing from the glint of black in his green eyes.

"You fear the wrong things," Sain said in a voice that was closer to a monster's interpretation of my father, the dark tones all wrong. It didn't fit him. It didn't fit him as I knew him, mumbling about how awesome he was and how he deserved to be treated like a god. The depth of his voice fit this confident villain just fine. "You put your trust in the wrong place. In the wrong master."

Sain stepped toward me, the sound of his foot against the cobbles more like a gunshot and I jerked. Another step, another shot, the sound more frightening given that the Vilỳ had reached us, but instead of ripping both of us to pieces they landed on the ground around him, on his shoulders, on the tree and bench, their tiny eyes looking at him as though they were worshiping him.

No, as though they were scared of him. I had fallen asleep wrapped in towels and the hot hands of my mate. Right then, I was alone.

Alone and freezing.

"I serve no master but myself and accept no master other than me. If you do not stand with me, then you will stand below this earth and be returned to the wells of Imdalind from which I was born," villain Sain said before taking another step, the heavy beat of foot against cobbles jerking me out of the nightmare and right back into my bedroom, to the too hard mattress and the scratchy blankets and to Ilyan who was trying to be quiet as he shifted through our tiny dresser in search of a shirt.

Now I knew where the heavy bangs in the dream had come from. Judging by the sock that was hanging out of one of the drawers, he had been searching in the dark for a while.

"Ilyan?" I mumbled, sleep heavy in my voice as I conjured a light, the golden orb flickering as though it was exhausted before igniting and floating to the ceiling.

"Shhh, my love. Go back to sleep, there is still time to rest," his whispered, his hand soft against my face as he pushed my slightly sweaty hair away, the bed compressing as he sat beside me. "You were dreaming."

"Nightmare, I think. You know how my mind plays with sights." The words were mumbled, but he caught the gist. I leaned into his hand like it was a lifeline, smelling the residue of magic that always followed him around. Except the ashy scent of his magic was more pungent than it had been.

"Ilyan?" I asked again, turning to the worry worn expression that he had tried to push away. Even with the weird shadows of my light against his face I saw it, the emotion laced with his magic as I pulled it out from where he had tried to tuck it away. "What's happened?"

"It's okay, Joclyn." Considering he was trying to block his thoughts as well as his emotions, I wasn't going to believe that for a second. "You haven't been asleep for long enough, only about thirty hours. You need more sleep, my love. Please trust that all is well and that we are handling it."

I leaned back on my pillow, although I didn't let go of his hand. I wasn't about to let him to get away with that and he knew it too. The hunt for a shirt was forgotten as he leaned over me, the ends of his hair tickling against my jaw. If he thought he was going to kiss me to shut me up, he had another thing coming.

"You know I would never do such a thing," he said, answering my thought.

"Then tell me what has happened."

He hesitated, his lips pulling into a tight line before he sat back, taking the tickling ends of his hair away. His hand did not leave mine.

"Is Thom okay?"

"Thom is fine. Dramin is fine," he answered hastily, giving my hand another squeeze before he left and went back to searching for a shirt. "Although there was an attack."

I sat up so fast that everything swam and dived, making the world look as though I had woken up in a kaleidoscope.

"What kind of attack?"

"We aren't sure. There were some Skřítek and a few chosen out on a training run to get food, some clothes. Medical supplies." Ilyan shook his head, pulling a long sleeved grey V-neck over his head. We had found it in a department store last week, along with the suit jacket he was now pulling on.

"Is everyone okay?"

"No." He didn't elaborate, but he didn't have to, I could see the shrouded hospital beds through his mind, the single image releasing all the worry, fear and pain that he had been trying to conceal out in a rush.

"We are trying to figure out what has happened," Ilyan continued, his voice strong even though everything inside of him was shaking. "But everyone's story is conflicting. There is only one constant, that the attack was from one man. A lone figure, wearing a dark black cloak."

Ice.

The world was made of ice. Even before he had said it the twist of cold had consumed me. I heard the words in his mind and my dream was suddenly screaming through me. Except it wasn't a dream. And it wasn't a nightmare.

It was sight.

Sight in a dream.

I guess it was possible.

I had seen three people run through a city with different looks on their face. Each one capable of taking down a few Skřítek on their own. Well, maybe not Sain. But with that darkness in his eyes... I guess anything was possible.

I didn't need a memory of that look, it was already making me wish the whole thing wasn't sight. I didn't think that look was possible for anyone, especially him and his sniveling.

Who knows, maybe it wasn't sight, maybe I was turning into some kind of prophet.

Okay, maybe not that. That was so much worse.

Ilyan's eyes met mine, my jaw dropped as much as my eyes popped, the kaleidoscope of the world picking up as Ilyan reran the images of the survivors returning to the cathedral, of Ryland with a lip punctured and bleeding.

"No!" I was on my feet, ready to throw on clothes and go find Sain, or whoever it was in the cloak. I was going with Sain. Wyn had told me she didn't own a cloak and I was going to treat that as gold.

"It wasn't Sain." Even Ilyan sounded disappointed in his proclamation.

"How do you know?"

"Because he--"

"I saw him." I interrupted, "In that sight. I saw him in a cloak. It had to be him."

"But that was Wyn?"

"And Ry, and Sain." I wrapped my hand around his bicep, I wasn't about to let him go and track her down. It couldn't be her. It couldn't. "I saw them all, just now. While I was sleeping."

Silence stretched between us, Ilyan's questions piling through his mind and drifting over to me in whispers that I couldn't quite make out. They merged with all of my unasked confusion until I was trapped in a symphony of sound and everything began spinning again. I sunk back down to the bed with a tiny sigh. Ilyan was right, I hadn't gotten enough sleep. It made the whole world fuzzy.

"A dream, Joclyn. It had to be a dream."

"It didn't feel like a dream. It felt real. Like a sight." I hated that I was second guessing myself, but even in the dream, as I had followed the horrifying faces of Wyn, Ry, and Sain it had felt a bit too real. A bit too much like a sight.

"I don't know what's real or not anymore, but we already know we can't trust Sain."

"That doesn't mean we can blame everything on him. We have to rule logically." Ilyan sighed, running his hand through his unbound hair before he sunk down onto the bed next to me, the mattress and frame groaning as I rocked into him. "We have to believe in the best of all of our subjects, Joclyn. Sain included."

It took everything in me to restrain the intense growl that wanted to escape me. The attempt earned me a tiny smile from Ilyan.

"There is to be a meeting with the hierarchy. Sain will be there. You may ask your questions there, and seeing as you are awake--" He let the invitation drip into the air as he stood, holding out his hand to me.

The world didn't spin quite as much as he pulled me to my feet, but the world wasn't any less of a spinning top. Except now everything was going topsy-turvy for a few different reasons.

"You should be there, as my queen," Ilyan's power infected his voice as he pulled me closer, lifting my hand as he gently kissed the back of it.

He was the only one who could call me Queen and not send my stomach into acrobatics. Unfortunately, it was still doing its flips, although this time it was for a different reason all together.

I couldn't see anything about this meeting ending well.

15

RYLAND

SHE HAD ASKED NO LESS than five times, but I wasn't going to let her heal me. My magic was doing fine on its own and while the cut above my eye was still bleeding most of the other injuries had already fully healed. I looked worse off than I was.

Which was possibly why Risha had asked to help me so many times. The bright concern in her eyes was the prelude for her asking again and I cut her off at the pass.

"I'm fine Risha," I said, dabbing the wet cloth above my eye and scooting my chair away from her. I hoped she didn't take that the wrong way, but I was feeling too shattered to let her magic mingle with mine right then. First, I didn't want to know how her magic would react to mine, and second, I was too desperate to feel her magic create some kind of party to allow that to happen.

I had already bonded myself to a future Queen, I was crazed enough that there was a good chance it could happen again. For all I knew, anytime my magic touched another's there would be some of explosion and instant bonding.

I knew better, but I wasn't going to risk it either way.

"I can heal myself, Risha, Scouts Honor," I smiled broadly and held my hand up in what I had assumed would be a show of good faith. Risha, however, looked to the ceiling, her mouth falling open in what I could have sworn was surprise.

I followed her gaze, my magic sparking in a panic as I half expected the hooded man to be hovering above us, just chilling in the basement kitchens, ready to drop down and end us right then.

My chair dropped to the floor with a loud clunk as I jumped to my feet, ready to attack, or strangle, or whatever was about to happen. But there was nothing there but some cracked plaster and a chandelier that was possibly older than Ilyan.

If anything was older than Ilyan.

"What is it?" My voice was strained, and I was sure I had ripped one of the still healing cuts on the back of my neck.

"I dunno. You are the one who was pointing at the ceiling."

"No, I was..." I stared at her. I had clearly misjudged the reach of that saying. "Never mind."

"Okay, Ry," She tried to make the same gesture back, but ended up flipping me off and broke out into deeper giggles when she realized what she had done.

"I believe your scouts had it wrong," she said through a laugh as the door to the hall swung open and a shuffle of heavy rubber soles ripped through the tinkling beauty of her laugh.

Tinkling beauty.

Yes, I had thought it.

Is that what you will think of when it is the sound of her bones scattering over the stone floor?

I picked my chair back up, falling into it with a groan

from too many body aches. Risha's chuckles faded away as Sain reached us.

"I sure hope you won with your face looking like that," Sain nodded toward the still healing cuts that lined my face, his voice more of a bark than usual.

He was clearly still pissed about the last meeting he had attended. I don't think he had even changed his clothes. He was still wearing the same suit, although parts of it were covered with a fine white powder, and a stain on the collar looked to be blood. But that could have been there before. Who knows where he had pulled the relic from.

I was pretty sure it was tweed, a fabric I hadn't seen anyone wear in my lifetime.

"I did. Knocked 'em right on their behind." It was the story I was supposed to stick to anyway.

Ilyan was pissed when Risha and I had relayed what happened and didn't want too many stories to get out in the hopes of keeping everything calm and orderly until we figured out what had happened. Luckily no one had died or the situation would be much worse.

As far as anyone other than Ilyan and those on the mission knew, I had defeated a few of Edmund's men. Knocked them into oblivion.

I may have saved everyone, but the exaggerated story was not recognition that I deserved.

Sain didn't seem to want to give it to me. His fuming turned into a steam engine with the slam of the door. Risha immediately jumping to her feet as Ilyan stormed his way in, followed closely by Wyn and Joclyn who looked half asleep.

"Glad to hear it, kid," Sain gave one irritated look to the King and his entourage before he plopped himself down in Risha's now empty seat, shifting it so that he kept his back directly toward Ilyan and the usual table they set the maps up on, which they were currently doing.

"You make sure Ilyan knows it, too. He can't keep treating people like he does, beating them down like dogs."

"Ilyan doesn't beat me down like a dog." I cut him off before he weaved his frustrated exaggerations into a web of disdain that even I couldn't escape from.

"Are you sure about that, Ryland? I would have said the same thing a few days ago. Yet, here I am." He gestured around himself as though he was bruised and tied to the chair.

"You aren't beaten down either," He snorted at that, his nostrils flaring until you could make out the nose hair from the four day growth of patchy facial hair that peppered his jaw and upper lip. "You are wearing the same suit."

I had said it in jest, I even lifted my eyebrow in false mockery, but Sain's eyes grew so dark that for a moment I expected him to go twist himself into a Drak. Instead, he unclipped the darn mug from where he had hung it on his belt and filled it with poison so thick I swear I could smell it.

"I do not think it is just that anymore," he murmured, his voice hidden underneath Ilyan's rough bark of command, something about a map of old Prague that was sending Risha out of the room so quick she was a blur.

I saw her go, trying to catch her in question, but she didn't even turn. She was gone to the other side of the room, and I was left sitting in the ancient wooden chairs, in the belly of an ancient city, with a man just as old staring at me.

I was wrong, there is plenty older than Ilyan.

Like this immortal with the darkness that was filling his penetrating stare. He had seen a fair bit more than my brother. Past. Present. All of it. Not that I needed a reminder.

"You know he has to keep everything in order, Sain. Keep

the newbies calm and not ready to run screaming madness through the city. That *was* quite the stunt you pulled at the fountain." I leaned closer to him, my hands clasped around the worn jeans on my knees as he drank slowly, he didn't look away from me.

"If you think that was nothing more than a stunt then myself, and your father, have done you an injustice."

"My father? What does Edmund have to do with this?"

"Everything. Isn't he at the center of this war? Isn't he the reason why Ilyan lords over everyone around him?" I could have sworn his eyes were growing darker. If he was going to call sight I wish he would get it over with. This intense staring match was making my neck prickle, and that was never a good thing for me.

"Ilyan is the King, Sain." I seemed to have said something wrong, his knuckles went white under the tightening grip on the mug, his still darkening eyes darting down to the liquid as it sloshed over the side of the cup. I hadn't even realized he was shaking.

I fought the urge to scoot away from the flying bits of poison, not that Sain would let any of it hit me. He had told me once that he had no interest in seeing what awaits me, and I was sure a drop of that stuff would trigger something, although perhaps not to the level of the fountain.

"And I am of the first." Each word hissed from between the clench in his teeth, it oozed into the air like a snake and twisted right over my soul as though they were going to infiltrate me.

The demon in him was shining through.

Are you sure it's his demon you are seeing, and not your own?

For once, the deranged voice in my head was right. It wasn't a demon. My father. I knew that look, I knew the depth of pain in his eyes and the shake of fear that was vibrating his bones. I felt it every time I battled against my own mind and what my father had done to me. I had seen him in the counsel hall when Joclyn was made queen, mumbling to himself, scowling at the girl as if it was someone else and not him that was seeing everything unfold.

He had told me I wasn't alone in my madness before. I knew exactly what he meant.

"How long have you been hearing his voice?" I leaned in with the whisper, bringing myself as close as I dared, seeing as the shake in his hands had become an earthquake.

It was good I hadn't got much closer, because the shake jumped like a jackrabbit when the man nearly jumped out of his chair. The wooden legs scraped against the stone floor with a sound that was only barely masked by the scrape of the door on Risha's return.

Joclyn and Ilyan may not have noticed the jump in the old man, but I was now on the receiving end of a glare from Wyn that with a tiny bit of spark could melt us both to the ground. I didn't need to deal with that when I was already trapped with a man who was having a nervous breakdown.

Wonderful. You can go mad together. Because of me. For me.

"It's okay. I've been there, obviously, I get it." I wasn't sure how to console anyone, I hadn't exactly been brought up in a consoling environment. On the team, we would smack each other's backs and tell our team mates to 'get back in it'. I wasn't quite sure that fit this situation, and judging by the way he was now staring at the water, a smack on the back could cause him to explode.

In the end, I awkwardly patted him on the knee, avoiding the massive wet spot on his tweed trousers and let him drain the Black Water from his mug in silence.

Get back in it.

I wasn't sure who had said that.

"How long have you known?" Sain asked, still looking at his mug with a look of shock I didn't think was possible for someone who could see the future.

It wasn't shock, however, his brow may be furrowed in confusion, but his eyes were narrowed in what I could only understand as hatred, his lips pulled into a line so tight it looked as if he was hiding a laugh.

"Since I got my brain on straight, I suppose." I was suddenly wishing I had something to occupy my hands with, but the only thing close enough was Sain's death mug. So instead I began writhing them, one over the other.

It was an old habit of my madness that wasn't welcome right now, and easily earned me a look from Risha.

Even from across the room, she was the one to notice, all the others were so absorbed in the maps and plans that they had forgotten we were here.

I gave her what I hoped was a reassuring smile and turned back to Sain, the darkness in his eyes was gone now, but that wasn't making his stare any less intense.

"Since the counsel, I saw you talking to yourself." He nodded at my response, and refilled his mug, giving me a break from his laser pointed stare.

"I see." He drained the mug again. "We should talk. Later. There is something I might need your help with."

"Ryland, if you could join us?" Ilyan's deep command pulled me from Sain's intensity like a slap, and this time I was the one to jerk. I jumped to my feet, Sain following me with his palm over his mug as he refilled it.

Joclyn stood by Ilyan, doing the same. If it wasn't like poison to me I would be interested to know what was in that stuff. The two of them were going at it like addicts.

"I know you weren't there when the man in the cloak

arrived, but I wanted to know if you had any indication of where they went?" Ilyan asked as I stepped up to the large piece of parchment and the littered mess of sticks and stones that was recreating the battle.

"Sorry, no," I said with a sigh, moving a rock a bit to the left, closer to where I had seen that poor Chosen cowering and crying behind the car. "There was a flash --"

"How do you know it was a guy?" Sain cut me off, stepping up to the table and placing his mug down with a loud thunk, drops flying out of it and discoloring the parchment.

I was surprised it didn't burn it away.

Everyone turned to look at him, Risha's eyes freezing on mine for half a second before continuing to join in the group stare down of Sain.

"Ryland filled me in," he added, but only Risha accepted that response. Wyn's scowl was about as deep as Joclyn's.

"Wonderful," I don't think I had even seen Joclyn force a smile, but it wasn't a good look for her.

"Did anyone see his face? Ryland didn't say, but if someone is attacking us I hope someone was able to see his face."

"We still aren't sure they had meant to attack us, Sain. It could simply be a case of crossed paths."

"But they attacked, so clearly they meant to attack us," Sain snapped at Ilyan, standing across from hi, as if to posture him. The visual was ridiculous, a tall powerful king and an old man with an unkempt beard and a tweed suit.

"Perhaps. Was Joclyn able to see? I assume she has tried." He lifted his mug to her, but it was not in a toast. "If not, I am sure I can gain you the answers that you seek."

Ilyan's jaw was now so tight there was a vein in his neck that looked about ready to pop. It was there and gone so fast that if it hadn't been so large it would have gone undetected. Even Joclyn was looking at him with a tad bit more worry than was normal, even for her.

"That is actually why we have asked you to join us, Sain. We would like your input, and we would love to have you join us again. If you will abide by the rules of the kingdom."

The darkness that I had seen in his eyes was gone, the hatred that I had watched him throw at Ilyan had left. He stood now, calm, his eyes green, the same man I had known in the dungeon. The same man who had saved so many.

It was devastating to see how much my father's voice, how much my father's madness, was affecting him. I had to help him.

"I would love to help. You know I am always here to serve you, my king."

ALSO BY REBECCA ETHINGTON

THE WORLD OF IMDALIND

THE CIRCUS OF SHIFTERS

Flame of the Phoenix, Book Four

The Dragon Queen Series

Rising Flame (coming 2019)

Books 2-4 TBA

THE OTHER WORLDS

The Through Glass Series

Book One: The Dark

Book Two: The Blue

Book Three: The Rose

Book Four: The Cut

Book Five: The Light (Coming 2019)

Book Six: The Ascended (Coming 2019)

Of River and Raynn, The Series

The Catalyst: Act One (Rereleases 2019)

The Requisite: Act Two (Coming 2019)

THE IMDALIND SERIES, BOOK SEVEN
THE FULL SERIES IS AVAILABLE NOW

www.ingramcontent.com/pod-product-compliance
Lightning Source LLC
Chambersburg PA
CBHW032007170626
46807CB00006B/2692